A King Production presents...

A Novel

JOY DEJA KING

Cover concept by Joy Deja King
Cover Model: Joy Deja King

Graphic design: www.anitaart79.wixsite.com/bookdesign
Typesetting: Anita J.

Library of Congress Cataloging-in-Publication Data;
King, Deja Joy
Stackin' Paper Part 6: a novel/by Joy Deja King
For complete Library of Congress Copyright info visit;
www.joydejaking.com Twitter: @joydejaking

A King Production
P.O. Box 912, Collierville, TN 38027

A King Production and the above portrayal logo are trademarks of A King Production LLC

This Book is Dedicated To My:

Family, Readers, and Supporters.
I LOVE you guys so much. Please believe that!!

—Joy Deja King

"Tell 'Em When I Die, Put My Money In The Grave. I Ain't About To Die With No Money, I Done Gave It..."

~Drake~

A KING PRODUCTION

Stackin
PAPER
VI

Money
In The
Grave...

A Novel

JOY DEJA KING

Chapter One

The Unthinkable

Nico, Supreme and Lorenzo pulled up to the detached single family home, with a private driveway on a quiet block of Clason Point section in the Bronx. It was pitch-black without any trace of someone being home.

"It look empty in that muthafucka. You sure this the address?" Supreme questioned when they arrived, parking across the street.

"Yep," Nico nodded, glancing down at the piece of paper Amir had given him. "It's late. The nigga probably sleep. We can walk in there, kill his ass and walk out," he shrugged.

"Fuck that! I want the nigga woke. Caleb snake ass is responsible for murdering Genesis. He deserve to feel the pain and know he about to die," Supreme seethed.

"I agree," Lorenzo chimed in. "Genesis went to bat for that young nigga. Showing him the ropes. Basically letting him run Philly and Caleb's punk ass was workin' for Arnez the entire time. Nah, won't be no dying in his sleep. He ain't gettin' off that easy."

"I feel you. We can wake him up," Nico agreed. "As long as the end result is that muthafucka dead...we good."

"Then let's go do this," Supreme said, turning off the car. The men retrieved their weapons getting out, heading towards the house.

"Oh shit!" Lorenzo mumbled stopping in the middle of the street.

"What is it?" Nico questioned.

"Somebody calling me," Lorenzo sighed, getting the phone from his coat pocket.

"Man, unless it's a burner we was supposed to leave all devices back at the office, so nobody could trace shit. And if they did, it wouldn't show this location," Supreme moaned.

"I hardly use this phone. I forgot I had it on

me. Don't nobody even really know this number," Lorenzo remarked.

"Turn that shit off," Nico shook his head.

"Hold up." The number was familiar to Lorenzo but it took him a minute to figure it out because this particular phone didn't have any contacts listed. "Oh shit, I think this Amir," Lorenzo said, finally recognizing the digits.

"He's probably checking to see if we found the spot and got rid of Caleb's ass yet," Supreme reasoned.

"You speak to Amir and we'll meet you inside," Nico said, as he and Supreme hurried off, ready to end Caleb's life.

"Cool." By the time Lorenzo answered the call, Amir had already hung up.

"I've tried every number you've given me and nobody is answering their phone," Amir told his father as they were driving over the RFK Triborough Bridge.

"Keep trying!" Genesis roared, pounding his fist down on the steering wheel. "They can't go to that fuckin' house."

Amir couldn't bring himself to tell his father

that he believed they might already be there. Right when he was about to try calling Supreme again, his phone started ringing. "It's Lorenzo!" Amir bellowed quickly answering. "Man, where ya at? We've been trying to reach you."

"Here at that spot and who is we?" Lorenzo questioned, right before he started getting a weak cell phone signal.

"Get away from there! It's a trap!" Amir shouted.

"Amir! Amir! Say that again!" Lorenzo yelled back. "We have a bad connection," he continued to yell, wondering if Amir could even hear him. He walked back across the street but there were lots of trees, so he headed towards the parked SUV, hoping to get better reception.

"Lorenzo, can you hear me now?!" Amir hollered in the phone.

"Yeah, a little better. Now what did you say?"

"I'm with..." Before Amir could continue, Genesis snatched the phone from his hand becoming agitated.

"L, it's me Genesis! Get the fuck away from that house right now, before all ya end up dead!" He barked.

As Lorenzo was turning around to yell for

Supreme and Nico to come back, he heard gunfire erupt and his phone said call failed.

"FUUUUUUUUUUUUUUUUUUUUUUUU CK!!!!!" Genesis's thunderous voice echoed through-out the truck. You would've thought the glass windows were about to shatter.

"Dad, what's wrong?!" Amir was panic-stricken.

"We gotta fuckin' hurry!" Genesis pressed down on the gas, pushing a hundred miles per hour in the dead of night. "I heard a bunch of gunshots and then the call dropped," he expressed frantically while trying to call Lorenzo back but it kept going straight to voicemail.

"Dad, watch out!" Amir swallowed hard as Genesis swerved, barely avoiding sideswiping another vehicle, as he made a last minute decision to take the next exit. He remembered a shortcut that would get them to the location within a few minutes.

"I got this! You just get the guns!" Genesis ordered. He had one of the best trap-car builders install a secret compartment in the majority of his vehicles. The intricate almost undetectable secret compartment could only be opened by hitting various buttons and switches in succession. It was installed behind the back seat of the truck.

It was rigged with a set of hydraulic cylinders linked to the vehicle's electrical system. The only way to make the seat slide forward and reveal its existence was by pressing and holding four switches simultaneously; two for the windows and two for the power door locks.

Amir did as his father instructed. His head was spinning, wondering if they were too late. He didn't want to believe the unthinkable. Because if Supreme, Nico and Lorenzo were dead, none of their lives would ever be the same again.

Chapter Two

Look Alive

Maverick's goons had moved Shiffon from the minivan to an abandoned warehouse. She was shackled to a steel pole, watching from a short distance as the men talked amongst each other.

They're probably deciding how to kill me right now. Please don't let them torture me first, Shiffon thought to herself, remembering all the targets she had brutalized before putting them out of their misery. When Shiffon became an assassin, she knew the potential hazards that came along with her job but ending up dead wasn't part of the equation. From where she was standing, it seemed inevitable.

Shiffon noticed Maverick dismissing his goons and making a phone call. The conversation seemed intense. She found herself staring at him and when Maverick's eyes locked with hers, Shiffon quickly turned away and put her head down. A few minutes later, he ended his call and came walking towards her.

"No reason to look away now," Maverick said placing his hand under Shiffon's chin and lifting her head up. "Are you ready to die?" with his other hand, he pulled a gun from the back of his pants and placed the tip against the temple of Shiffon's head.

Shiffon closed her eyes, fighting back tears. Part of her didn't feel like she had the right to cry or beg for her life. She had been the one holding the trigger so many times, she needed to take her bullet like a real G.

"I get it. I know the game. I guess it's my time, so go ahead and pull the trigger," Shiffon stated gravely. From the side of her eye, she saw Maverick's finger gripping the trigger and then she heard the click. Shiffon gasped then cried out believing she had crossed over to the afterlife.

"I guess you were wrong. It ain't yo' time to

die just yet," Maverick said, moving Shiffon's hair from over her eye. "You don't have to hold back the tears. I already seen you cry."

"Is that what you want me to do? Beg for my life. Tell you how sorry I am?" Shiffon's voiced cracked.

"I don't want you to tell me shit that you don't mean. You a killer. I wouldn't believe nothing you say anyway."

"I'm a killer but so are you. The weapon I use is typically a gun and yours is drugs. What's the difference?"

"There's a huge fuckin' difference. I give people freedom of choice. They choose to use drugs. You didn't give my muthafuckin' men no choice when you and yo' girls murdered them in front of my eyes and took my mother!" Maverick barked, raising his hand to slam the gun in Shiffon's head but he stopped himself.

"I'm sorry!" Shiffon cried out. "But please know this, I was never gonna hurt your mother."

"You a fuckin' lie!" Maverick spit.

"It's true. Initially I wasn't gonna take the job because I didn't want to kill somebody's mother. But they were adamant Genesis had no intentions of ever killing her and didn't want her harmed in any way."

"Whatever." Maverick shook his head as if he wasn't believing anything Shiffon said.

"It's true!" Shiffon implored. "I'm not just-ifying what I do for a living but the people I'm hired to kill are more sinners than saints."

"We all sinners, so what's yo' point?"

"The point is, killing your mother was never part of the plan. I put that on everything. Genesis was trying to save his daughter's life. He was willing to do just about anything except kill your mother and that's the truth."

"Maybe you're right but that don't give him a pass and you neither. He hired you to kill my crew and he will suffer the consequences. I can promise you that."

"And what about me? Am I gonna suffer too?"

"Of course you are but I have other plans for you first."

Maverick locked eyes with Shiffon and there was no denying the mutual attraction. Their sexual chemistry was only heightened by Maverick's rage towards the woman who he partially blamed for killing his men. He hated himself for wanting her but rejecting his urge to have Shiffon was becoming increasingly difficult, even for a man as methodical as Maverick.

"What tha fuck was that?!" Supreme was breathing rapidly, after him and Nico took cover. When they were ambushed with a barrage of bullets, storming inside the house was their only option.

"Man, they got me," Nico mumbled. At first Supreme couldn't understand what Nico said because his voice was low and his words were unintelligible. It wasn't until he noticed him holding the side of his stomach and blood soaking through his shirt, did Supreme realize Nico had been shot.

"Gotdammit!" Supreme fumed, rushing to Nico's side. The men had a long standing aversion for each other but seeing his onetime rival hurt, had Supreme in his feelings. "Nico, don't move," he said. His initial reaction was to get Nico to the car and take him to the hospital but Supreme could still hear the gunfire outside. It wasn't safe for them to come out but Nico was also in dire need of medical attention.

"This shit hurt." Nico's eyes were a bit droopy. He was leaning against the wall, holding his side. Supreme zoomed in on the injury. The gunshot wound didn't have a big hole, so he knew Nico was shot by a handgun. Not to say they weren't dangerous but handguns produce significantly slower velocity projectiles than say a rifle, and therefore typically cause less severe injuries.

"You need to sit down," Supreme said trying to assist Nico. He knew gunshot wounds to the abdomen bleed more quickly if the legs are elevated, making it harder for the person to breathe. "We gotta slow the bleeding down." Supreme glanced around wondering if there was a bathroom nearby that had some towels. But it was dark and he didn't want to waste unnecessary time. With a swiftness, Supreme took off his shirt, balled it up and used it to seal Nico's wound. He leaned down hard on it, hoping the pressure would help minimize the bleeding.

"Man, you can stop tryna save my life. I know you don't like my ass and I don't like you either," Nico cracked. His voice becoming sluggish.

"Nah nigga. You ain't about to die on my watch. Precious would never forgive me. She'd swear down I let the shit happen on purpose." Supreme tried to keep a jokey vibe, not wanting to reveal how concerned he was as he checked Nico's pulse. It was weak and Supreme worried he was suffering from internal bleeding too. If so,

Nico wouldn't survive much longer without the proper treatment at a medical facility.

Genesis slowed down as he turned the corner of the street and switched off the headlights. He could see a few men across the street, near the house busting shots in the direction of Supreme's truck and someone was returning fire but they couldn't see who it was. Genesis put the SUV in reverse and parked the car out of view.

"We're gonna go around to the back of the house and take out the muthafuckas shooting at Supreme's truck. Anybody who ain't, Nico, Lorenzo or Supreme, just kill 'em. We ain't asking no questions. You understand?" Genesis wanted confirmation from his son.

"I understand but you don't think we should wait for backup? Our men should be pulling up any minute," Amir reminded his father.

"We can't wait for backup! My niggas might be dead by the time my men arrive. We gotta handle this shit ourselves. Now are you ready, Amir? If not, you stay in the fuckin' car, cause I ain't got time to babysit you," Genesis made clear. He checked to make sure the three guns he was bringing were fully loaded. He had one in each hand and another in the back of his pants.

"I'm ready, dad." Amir nodded. He was nervous but would never admit it to his father. With the lavish lifestyle he lived and all the riches he had, Genesis was still a street nigga at heart. His son on the other hand, was smart but far from fearless. Amir came from privilege, which meant he never had to struggle. But he admired his father and whatever he needed to do in order to gain his respect, then so be it. If that meant jumping out the truck with guns blazing, then Amir was on board.

"You stay behind me but watch and lookout for anything that don't seem right," Genesis stressed to his son. "Again, if it ain't Supreme, Nico or Lorenzo, shoot to kill the muthafuckas," he reiterated. "We'll figure the other shit out later."

"Got you." Amir nodded his head, maintaining a brave face. He trailed slightly behind his father. The houses were spread somewhat far apart, so he wanted to make sure he could see their surroundings. Amir was literally making sure he had his father's back.

Genesis suddenly stopped and turned back at Amir. He put his finger to his mouth, motioning his son to be quiet. Then he pointed towards a man who was kneeling down near the back entrance of the house, looking through a window with his gun positioned on the glass. Genesis waved his arm, letting Amir know to cover him as he snuck up behind the enemy. When Amir got in position, he could see two other men exchanging gunfire. For a brief second, he caught a glimpse of Lorenzo when he came from around the truck to return fire. That's when he realized, Nico and Supreme must be inside the house.

"Get him, dad." Amir muttered as Genesis got closer to his target.

Genesis was trying to keep his presence unknown but had to speed up his pace before the shooter pulled the trigger. He could tell the man had zoomed in on his target and was ready to fire. In his rush to stop him, Genesis sprinted up the stairs leading to the back entrance and when he stepped on the third stair, it squeaked loudly.

"What tha fuck!" The shooter glanced back to see where the noise was coming from. He immediately swung his gun at Genesis but Genesis used his elbow to knock it away from his face. But the shooter still had enough time to get a shot off, which brought unwanted attention.

"Shit! Here comes the cavalry," Amir shook his head, seeing the other two men rushing towards the back with their guns raised. He came running out from behind the trees, sneaking up on them. Amir was a bit rusty because he had participated in very few gun battles. He discharged a few wild shots, luckily a bullet connected with one of the men. Hitting him in the leg, causing him to fall down in the grass. Once Amir warmed up, that aim got better and he was able to put both the men down permanently.

Genesis's situation turned into a minor scuffle but he quickly gained the upper hand. By the time Amir reached the stairs to assist his father, Genesis had already put two shots in the man's head, leaving him for dead.

"Dad, Lorenzo was the one exchanging fire with those men I just killed. I'm thinking Nico and Supreme are inside the house," Amir told his father.

"You go around front and check on Lorenzo. I'll go in the house and make sure Supreme and Nico are okay," Genesis said calling out their names. He knew both men were more than likely armed and didn't want to go inside and they mistakenly kill him.

He banged on the back door and yelled

out their names again. "Supreme! Nico! It's me Genesis!"

It took a minute but then he heard what sounded like Supreme calling out. Genesis could hear footsteps running towards the door.

"Nigga, I thought I was losing my fuckin' mind! You supposed to be dead," Supreme announced when he opened the door. "You can explain that shit to me later. We gotta get Nico to the hospital. He got shot. It's bad."

"Fuck! That explains why you ain't got on no shirt," Genesis remarked following Supreme to where Nico was laying on the floor. He looked halfway dead, which shook Genesis to the core. Supreme's white shirt was now bloody red.

"Is it okay to take him out front?" Supreme wanted to know. "I ain't think them bullets was gonna ever stop ringing."

"It's safe out there," Genesis assured Supreme as the two men lifted Nico up from the floor and carried him outside to the truck.

"Damn," both Amir and Lorenzo shook their heads when they laid eyes on Nico. It was bad and they knew it.

My nigga Nico ain't gonna survive this... Lorenzo thought to himself. Although no one wanted to admit it and refused to utter the words out loud, secretly they all shared the same sentiment.

Chapter Three

Share My World

Every time the phone would ring, Precious was praying it was good news. The last she heard, Supreme, Nico and Lorenzo were still missing and on top of that, her worse fears had been confirmed. Aaliyah was the one who had Justina's baby kidnapped and was now on the run. *Things can't possibly get anymore chaotic,* she thought to herself answering the phone.

"Hello."

"Guess who's back..." The familiar voice said cheerfully. Precious had to catch her breath.

This was the one call she was never expecting to receive.

"Skylar! Is it really you?!" Precious gasped.

"Yep, it's me. I wanted to call you sooner but I needed to get my strength up," Skylar explained.

"How long have you been out of your coma?"

"A few days now but when I initially woke up, I was in an out. Today is the first time I'm feeling normal again."

"This is the best news. I needed this. So who else knows?"

"Only my mother. They called her when I woke up and she brought Genevieve. Precious, I thought I would never see my daughter again." Skylar's voice cracked as she fought back tears.

"I know but all of our prayers have been answered. You survived and now Genevieve has her mother back."

"True but unfortunately she doesn't have a father," Skylar stated sadly.

"You don't know...your mother didn't tell you?" Precious questioned.

"Tell me what?" Skylar sounded confused. "Honestly, we didn't do much talking. Like I said, I've been out of it. All I wanted was to see my baby's face."

"That's understandable." Precious hesitated.

She wasn't sure if this was something she should tell Skylar on the phone or in person. "Genesis is Genevieve's father," she blurted out, believing her friend deserved to hear the truth and also get some good news.

"Don't play with me, Precious." Skylar's tone switched from sad to stern and serious.

"I would never play about my Goddaughter. That beautiful baby girl has a father. His name is Genesis and he loves her so much."

"Genesis knows?"

"Of course! Once Genesis found out the truth, he moved heaven and earth to bring you both home safely."

Skylar stopped fighting back her tears and began to bawl her heart out over the phone. "I knew in my heart Genesis was her father. Only he could've given me a baby that perfect," she cried. "How did he find out the truth?"

"I'm not sure," Precious lied. "But when you speak to Genesis make sure you ask."

"You know I will. I guess I should call him."

"I think that's a good idea."

"So when am I gonna see you? I would love to have some company since the doctor said they're going to keep me here for another week or so," Skylar complained.

"I'll be there later on today and I'll bring some of your favorite treats."

"You're the best, Precious. I can't wait to see you!" Skylar beamed.

"Ditto. Now go call yo' baby daddy, girl!" Precious laughed before ending their call.

"Supreme, I don't know how much longer I can keep lying to Precious. She can be very..." Amir seemed to be struggling to find the right word.

"Difficult," Supreme said, trying to help Amir out.

"I was thinking more like intimidating."

"I guess in your case I can see that," Supreme shrugged. "But listen, we all agreed not to tell Precious anything until we know what's gonna happen with Nico."

"I think we pretty much know, he's not gonna make it. Does it really make sense to prolong the inevitable. Precious needs to know, so she can tell Aaliyah. Angel needs to know too. They should be able to say goodbye to their father," Amir pleaded.

"I've never told anyone this and if you repeat it, I'ma say you need to shut the fuck up because you talk too much," Supreme warned Amir. "Nico has been a thorn in my flesh for too many fuckin' years but I respect him because he a real ass nigga. So don't you dare count that man out. He ain't dead yet. The doctor said, they gonna perform one more surgery."

"I know but..."

"But nothing!" Supreme barked, cutting Amir off. "His eyes might be closed and he can't speak to us but trust, Nico still fightin' for his life. If only so he can come back and fuck wit' me," Supreme quipped. "Ain't no way that nigga gon' let me outlive him. So you handle Precious. Be there for her. I'ma stay at this hotel until Nico pulls through," he proclaimed staring out the window. "He has to pull through." Supreme put his head down and prayed.

"You tellin' me all three of the men you hired are dead?! Nigga, is you stupid!" Maverick barked at his man Cam. "If our men dead, then at least tell me Genesis's partners are dead too?"

Cam let out a disappointing sigh. "Nah. One might got hurt but I ain't got no confirmation on that. I know this ain't what you wanted to hear but…" He said with a shrug of the shoulders, not having an explanation.

"I can't believe this dumb shit." Maverick shook his head pissed but not willing to give up. "You still got eyes on them?"

"They've all gone ghost except for Genesis. But that nigga rolling wit' a crew of security. Ain't nobody gettin' to him," Cam revealed.

"Then we start going down the list of people he care about. At least one of them will be left exposed. And when they are, we go in for the kill." Maverick was determined to make sure Genesis felt his wrath. "And don't fuck this up, Cam or I'm coming for you," he threatened.

"It's handled," Cam promised. "What about the chick Shiffon…what you want me to do wit' her?"

"Let me worry about her. You focus on Genesis. Just make sure you keep a guard posted outside her door at all times. You can go now." Maverick dismissed Cam still seething. He then headed upstairs to check on his prisoner. A week ago he had Shiffon moved from the abandoned warehouse, to one of his cribs in the outskirts of Philly. He was still debating what to do with her. She was supposed to be dead by now but Maverick kept trying to find reasons to keep her alive. As he got closer to the bedroom, he could hear music playing. ***Nobody Else*** by Summer Walker

Nobody else but you
Nobody else would make this move
Nobody else had a clue
What I could do, what I could do?

The right amount of love, right amount of thrust
Right amount of dick
Right amount of slap me up, I think I'm throwing a fit
Right amount of rough play, right amount of talking to me
Oh yeah

Feel it in my heart, feel it in my soul
Feel like in my bod-, my body, baby...

"You startled me!" Shiffon jumped, when she realized Maverick was standing in the doorway. Her body was still wet from just getting out the shower. "How long have you been standing there?" she asked turning down the music.

"Not long. I haven't come through in a couple days and wanted to make sure you wasn't in here plotting on how to escape," Maverick remarked, glancing around the room before closing the door.

"Look all you like, you won't find nothing. There's no windows, you left the bare minimum in here but I won't complain. At least I can listen to music, watch television and of course I'm not dead," Shiffon said tightening the towel around her body.

"How badly do you want to stay alive?"

"Is that some sort of trick question? You know I don't wanna die. I'm trying to figure out the reason I'm not dead yet. Unless this is part of your game plan. To mentally torture me because at any moment when that door opens, it could be my time to die."

"I have a proposition for you. One I advise you to take."

"What is it?" Shiffon wasn't sure what offer Maverick would make but to stay alive, she was willing to do just about anything.

"I want you to kill Genesis. His life to save yours."

Shiffon sat down on the edge of the bed. This wasn't the proposal she was expecting Maverick to make.

"Is there a reason you not jumping to accept

my offer? I mean this is what you do for a living. You a hired killer...an assassin. This should be an easy yes for you?" Maverick reasoned.

"When I'm hired to do a job, I know the risk. I'm not gonna turn around and go after a previous client because the dirt I did comes back to bite me in the ass," Shiffon scoffed. "Genesis paid me in full for my services. He honored our agreement and I'ma do the same. So no, I won't be killing him because you escaped death and came back to seek revenge. If that's what you want from me, then you should go ahead and kill me now."

"You sure that's the choice you wanna make? Give up yo' life for a muthafucka who wouldn't think twice about taking yours," Maverick spit.

"This not about what Genesis would or would not do. Believe it or not, even though I kill people for a living, there are certain rules to this game I follow. Killing a previous client who paid me in full and did absolutely nothing wrong, is against all the rules."

"You serious about this?" Maverick was now standing within a few feet of Shiffon. He gave her a menacing stare and she knew he was about to break her neck but she didn't back down from her stance.

"Yes, I am. If that's the only way you'll let me stay alive, then I might as well go ahead and die. Because there is no way I'll be willing to do what you're asking. It will just be a waste of both of our time."

Shiffon let out a deep sigh anticipating her demise. She didn't want to die but knew it was inevitable at this point. Maverick no longer had any use for her and she had no interest in pretending she was down with his bullshit. It was obvious to Shiffon that Maverick was a very smart man and trying to con him, would do more harm than good. She hoped by being honest, he would end her life quickly and spare her a torturous death.

"You can get dressed now." Maverick told Shiffon, then turned to leave.

"I don't wanna get dressed so you can take me somewhere to die. I'd rather you kill me now and get it over with," Shiffon lamented.

"I'm not gonna kill you. I'm letting you go." Maverick stated to Shiffon's disbelief.

"What...but why?" her face was filled with bewilderment. This had to be a joke but Maverick looked dead ass serious which had Shiffon even more puzzled.

"You ain't leaving me much of a choice. If

you showing respect to the game, then I have to do the same. My beef is wit' Genesis. You were just hired to do a job. You not part of his family or inner circle. Hurting you, won't hurt him," Maverick acknowledged.

"So just like that, you're gonna let me walk outta here?" Shiffon felt there had to be a catch.

"Yes. I'm confident you'll stay in yo' place and won't try to retaliate against me. Besides, I know where your mother and little brother live." Maverick put Shiffon on notice.

"I'm sure you do but I'm surprised you trust that at some point I won't wanna make sure you're dead."

"Are you tryna talk yo' way back into being killed?" Maverick questioned with a raised eyebrow.

"No but can you blame me for being suspicious."

"Listen, I gave you a legitimate reason why I'm lettin' you go. I'm also sure one day you'll repay the favor, for me allowing you to keep yo' life." Maverick stated with certainty.

"I think there's also another reason you're keeping me alive. And it's much more personal."

"Personal in what way?" Maverick seemed intrigued.

Shiffon rose from the bed and walked over to Maverick. He had his hand on the knob, about to open the door. She placed her hand on top of his. "In the line of work I'm in, I have to be able to read people very quickly. Am I wrong about you?" she questioned, putting even less space between them. If they were any closer, their mouths would be touching.

"You don't wanna do this." His eyes were flashing danger but Shiffon ignored the warning.

"I wouldn't be standing here if I didn't. I wanted this from the moment I felt your hands all over my body." Shiffon leaned forward putting her lips on his for a brief second. When Maverick didn't rebuff her advances, Shiffon went in again with much more aggression. Her follow up kiss was anything but fleeting and Maverick responded accordingly. His hand was off the doorknob and undoing the towel wrapped around Shiffon's body. There was nothing sweet or subtle about their interaction. Their exchange was passionate and intense.

"I been wanting you so fuckin' bad." Maverick speaking those words in Shiffon's ear, instantly got her open.

"I want you too," she whispered back between kisses as Maverick's strong arms lifted Shiffon's naked body up. She wrapped her legs around his waist, without their lips ever being apart. They both seemed to be lost in the moment but their lust once again took over. Maverick laid Shiffon down on the bed and began to take off his clothes but impatience got the best of her. She decided to help speed up the process, ready to skip straight to the climax.

Shiffon damn near ripped the V-neck t-shirt off Maverick's wide strong shoulders. She paused for a moment and glanced up at him. He had this perfectly chiseled face yet staring down at her with these soft eyes, inviting Shiffon into his world and she welcomed the invitation. She slid her finger down the ripples in his etched abs. The precision of Maverick's torso would have one believe he was doing reverse crunches on a daily. But once his pants came down, the only muscle that truly mattered had Shiffon's full intention. She leaned in to taste his enticing tool but he stopped her, wanting to taste the sweetness between her thighs instead.

Maverick deliberate caresses with his tongue had Shiffon's wet pussy throbbing. She pressed her nails deep into his back, gripping his skin as she bit down on her bottom lip. Just when Shiffon believed she reached the peak of euphoria, Maverick replaced his tongue action with his well-equipped dick. He took his time sliding into her wetness, wanting to bring Shiffon pleasure instead of pain.

"Damn, you feel so good," he moaned, wanting to collapse inside the pussy.

I couldn't possibly feel as good as you, Shiffon said to herself, thinking she was getting hypnotized with each stroke. But she refused to allow herself to become fixated on how Maverick's sex game had her open. Shiffon wanted to savor every second of their forbidden sexual tryst.

Chapter Four

Dangerous Game

When Skylar opened her eyes and saw Genesis standing in her room with a beautiful bouquet of flowers, she thought her heart would melt.

"I wasn't expecting for you to come so soon," she smiled, sitting up in the hospital bed. "And those flowers are gorgeous. I'm guessing they're for me," Skylar blushed.

"Of course there for you," Genesis said, placing the vase on a table next to her. "How are you feeling...can I get you anything?"

"Actually, I'm feeling great," Skylar beamed.

Taking in the sweet vanilla scent of the orchids and the damask fragrance courtesy of the velvety rose petals.

"You look great too," Genesis smiled, sitting down in the chair near her bed. "But it's good to hear you're feeling great."

"Oh please. I definitely don't look great but I appreciate you pretending that I do," Skylar said coyly. "I've had a chance to look in the mirror since I woke up from my coma. I need a facial, my eyebrows done…the works!" She laughed.

"I'm not pretending. You've always been a natural beauty, Skylar," Genesis stated sweetly. "But I get it. I tell you what. After you get discharged, I'll schedule an appointment for you to be pampered at the best spa in the city."

"You've always been such a generous man," Skylar stated, reflecting back on how good Genesis had been to her, even after Talisa was once again in his life.

"This doesn't qualify as generous. With everything you've been through, it's the least I can do. You deserve so much more. Skylar, I should've…"

"You don't have to say it, Genesis." Skylar stopped him mid-sentence, having a good idea what was coming next.

"Yes I do. I'll never forgive myself for ever doubting Genevieve was mine. I'm the reason you almost died."

"No you're not! The only person you should be blaming is Arnez." Before Skylar could continue, she glanced over at her flowers and then fidgeted with the bed sheets nervously. "You had every right to take a paternity test. I slept with another man. When I found out I was pregnant, I prayed you were the father of my baby. But I should've been honest with you from jump," she reasoned.

"No. I shoulda never done the test in the first place. From the moment I held Genevieve in my arms, after delivering her, I knew she was my daughter. Even when the paternity test came back that I wasn't the father, deep down I knew it wasn't true. I made the mistake of listening to my head instead of following my heart," Genesis divulged.

"I felt the same way. But how can you dispute DNA. Once I got the results back, I told myself I had to accept the truth and move on. Wishful thinking wouldn't change the results of the paternity test. Guess I was wrong," Skylar giggled.

"Indeed," Genesis nodded with a slight laugh.

"When Precious told me you were Gene-vieve's father, she said you should be the one to tell me how the truth came out. So tell me Genesis, how did you learn the results were wrong?"

Genesis let out a deep sigh. He had been dreading having this conversation but knew Skylar deserved the truth. "The results were changed."

"Changed...on purpose?" Skylar raised an eyebrow, taken aback by what Genesis said.

"Yes," he nodded.

"By who?"

Genesis swallowed hard. He tried to bury the thought deep in his head because every time he thought about what his son did, he became enraged. "Amir."

"Amir is the reason my daughter was denied her father for all those months." Skylar's eyes watered up. "I knew when Talisa came back into your lives, he preferred me not being around but never did I imagine Amir would try to per-manently erase our daughter from your life." Skylar kept shaking her head, horrified by what Genesis had told her.

"I know. I don't think I will ever forgive Amir for what he did," Genesis conceded. He hated having so much animosity towards his own flesh and blood but he couldn't deny how he felt.

"Listen, I don't want to dwell on what Amir did. God has given me a second chance to be a Mother to Genevieve and allow our daughter to have a relationship with you. I rather count my blessings instead of being angry at Amir or anyone else," Skylar smiled.

"You're truly an amazing woman and our daughter is blessed to have a Mother like you. I know you were almost killed trying to shield Genevieve from harm and I promise to protect both of you for the rest of my life," Genesis vowed, as he held Skylar's hand.

Precious detested feeling powerless. She missed her husband but there was nothing she could do about his predicament. As far as she knew, Supreme, Nico and Lorenzo were all still missing. Refusing to remain stagnant, Precious put all her energy into something she had control over... finding her daughter. Following her gut instinct, she decided to place a call to the one person she believed Aaliyah would've been in contact with.

"Hi Angel, this is Precious. I hope I didn't catch you at a bad time."

"No of course not. Is everything okay?" Angel asked. Precious rarely, if ever called Nico's youngest daughter, so she wasn't surprised by her question.

"Yes, everything is fine but I'm having a little difficulty getting in touch with Aaliyah. Have you spoken to her?"

"Actually, I spoke to her a few days ago."

"Really? Did she tell you where she was?"

"She mentioned she'd be doing some traveling and I might not be able to reach her but she'll be in touch. Is something wrong?"

"There's a minor issue regarding Supreme and I wanted to let her know but her cell keeps going straight to voicemail. I was hoping maybe you could be some help," Precious sighed, feeling she had reached another dead end.

"When Aaliyah first called, it was from her cell but we were getting poor reception so she called me back from another number. I think it was a landline. Let me check my recent calls and see if the number is still there," Angel said. There was a brief moment of silence. "Sorry Precious, it's no longer in my phone but I do remember it being a 913 area code."

"Are you sure it was 913?"

"I'm positive. It stuck out to me because I've

never gotten a call from that area code before. I wish I could be more help."

"Angel, you've been a tremendous help. Thanks so much!"

"You welcome!"

"Oh, and Angel if you hear from Aaliyah before I reach her, don't let her know we spoke. I don't won't her worrying about Supreme."

"Of course. I hope everything works out."

"Me too," Precious said, before hanging up. "Do you know what area code 913 is?" she asked Amir.

Per Supreme's orders, Amir had been spending a great deal of time with Precious. Plus, he was also concerned about Aaliyah and Justina. Amir still cared deeply for both of his exes.

"913...nope, not off the top of my head but Siri is our friend," Amir joked, instantly getting the answer. "No way Aaliyah is in Kansas. There's nothing glam girl about that place."

"It's probably the exact reason Aaliyah chose to hide out there. Call your private investigator and have him check all flights and hotels for the past couple weeks in Kansas and the surrounding area. Angel spoke to her a few days ago, so there's a chance she's still there," Precious hoped.

"I'm on it."

Precious wasn't sure what she hated more. Knowing her daughter could spend the rest of her life on the run, or if she got caught, she could spend years in prison. She believed there was only one option, find Aaliyah before she ruined her life.

Shiffon woke up the next morning in Maverick's arms. She thought she would feel regret about them having sex but she felt the exact opposite. Shiffon reveled in their night of passion. He was the first man she'd been with since her ex Dino got locked up and it was fucking amazing. Their sexual chemistry was so intense, you would've thought they were making love like a young newlywed couple. As much as Shiffon wanted to stay in bed with Maverick, she knew it was time for her to go.

"Where you going?" Maverick mumbled when he saw Shiffon getting out of bed.

"You looked so peaceful laying there. I didn't mean to wake you." Shiffon bent down kissing him on the lips.

"Get back in bed."

"I can't."

"Why not?" Maverick wanted to know.

"I've been MIA for a minute. I'm sure my family and friends are worried sick about me. If I don't make contact soon, they'll probably call the police, if they haven't already. Then they'll start asking questions that I don't want to answer. And I'm sure you don't want me to either," Shiffon explained.

"True but you can just call them. Let 'em know you good," Maverick suggested.

"You know it's not that simple."

"Don't make me hold you hostage again," he joked, pulling Shiffon back down in bed. Sprinkling kisses all over her neck, breasts, down to her navel. "I don't want you to go."

Shiffon stopped Maverick before his warm tongue touched the inside of her clit. She knew if he went any further, there would be no resisting him. "Don't do this," she pleaded. "I really do need to check up on my Mother and little brother. This is the longest I've ever gone without speaking to them."

"Okay. I'll let you go but only if you promise to come back." Maverick stated, keeping Shiffon in his grip.

"I promise." Shiffon lifted Maverick's face up and kissed him again. "You didn't think I was gonna let you get rid of me so easily," she teased.

"Nah. Not the way you was sayin' my name last night," he cracked.

"Whatever!" Shiffon laughed, picking up one of the pillows on the bed and playfully hitting Maverick over the head with it. "I heard you calling out my name a few times too."

"No doubt. That pussy something special. So don't get brand-new and start denying me," Maverick grinned, giving Shiffon another kiss before they both got up. "When should I be expecting you back?"

"Tomorrow night."

"Why so long?" Maverick questioned.

"You do realize how long I've been missing. I'm still tryna figure out what I'ma tell people," Shiffon sighed thinking about Caleb.

"Tell 'em the truth."

"Excuse me?"

"You were kidnapped and you escaped. You can give them the previous location I had you stashed at. I won't be using it again."

"That's actually a pretty good idea," Shiffon acknowledged.

"I've learned that when you lie, if one part of the statement is true, most people will believe and accept the entire story as true."

"I'll keep that in mind when I'm interrogating you," Shiffon winked.

"I know what you do and you know first-hand what I'm capable of. To keep the peace, I think we should put a strict limit on any sort of interrogations."

"I guess that means, you don't wanna tell me what you have planned for the rest of the day." Shiffon cut her eyes at Maverick.

"Nope. The less you know, the more surprised you can genuinely be when shit get real out here."

Shiffon didn't even want to know what Maverick had planned because she knew none of it was good and more than likely involved Genesis. Although she never met him personally, she respected how he handled business. Shiffon didn't want anything bad to happen to the man who had paid her handsomely, to handle a couple jobs for him. But it wasn't her place to tell Maverick what he should and shouldn't do.

Based on what transpired, he had every right to seek retribution against Genesis. He was responsible for having his entire crew wiped out and his Mother being kidnapped. Still, Shiffon was torn. She had this burning desire to see if the mind blowing sex the two shared, could turn into something more. But she also wanted to be loyal to Caleb and Genesis. Shiffon was playing a very dangerous game that had the potential of turning fatal for everyone involved.

Chapter Five

Woman To Woman

When Caleb arrived at the rooftop lounge Assembly at The Logan hotel he was stressed and relieved at the same time. He also had a ton of questions and started spitting them before Shiffon could even greet him with a hello.

"Yo where you been and why you just now returning my phone calls? I done left you a shit-load of messages. I thought something happened to you."

"Caleb, sit down," Shiffon said taking his hand. Seeing this tall, young, well dressed, good looking black man, speaking in a somewhat aggressive tone, had everyone's attention which Shiffon wanted to avoid. "I ordered us a bottle of wine. Why don't you have a drink and enjoy this enviable city view," she proposed looking out at downtown Philly.

"I don't want no drink," Caleb scoffed, pushing the glass away. "And I done seen this fuckin' view a million times. I just need you to answer my question," he demanded.

Shiffon took a sip of her wine and let out a deep sigh. "I was kidnapped."

"What?!" Caleb belted. His eyes widened. He had a mixture of concern and anger on his face.

"Calm down," Shiffon insisted in a low tone. "I had us meet here because I figured we wouldn't see anyone we know and have some privacy. You bringing us unwanted attention is defeating the purpose," she said shaking her head.

"My fault." Caleb sat back in his chair, rubbing his hand over his chin. He exhaled, knowing he needed to chill. "Who kidnapped you?"

"I'm not sure," Shiffon lied. I was in the car, headed to my hotel and some men blocked me in. I was dragged out of my car, threw me in a back of a van and blindfolded me. They had me stashed someplace on Clearfield St."

"You been there all this time?" Caleb leaned forward staring keenly into Shiffon's eyes as if searching for answers.

"Yes. I was finally able to escape late last night. The only reason I got away, is because some niggas ran up in the spot. Not sure if was a robbery or what. I hid in the bedroom closet where they kept me. Once the gunfire stopped, I stayed in there for at least another hour before getting the hell out."

"Yo, that's fuckin' crazy. Man, I'm glad you a'ight," Caleb said, reaching out and gently stroking Shiffon's hand. "They didn't hurt you did they, or..."

"No I wasn't hurt and if you were going to ask if I was sexually assaulted, the answer is no. I'm not sure what their endgame was but luckily I got out before finding out."

"I bet that nigga Maverick was behind that shit!" Caleb fumed.

"You think? You all haven't caught him yet?" Shiffon questioned like she didn't already know the answer.

"Hell fuckin' no. That nigga tried to take out Genesis's partners and almost succeeded. Maverick need to go!" Caleb seethed. "That was one of the reasons I was blowing up yo' phone.

When I got word what went down wit' Genesis's people, I figured yo' life might be in danger too."

"You're probably right. Thank goodness I got away."

"Do you remember exactly where that muthafucka had you stashed?" Caleb wanted to know.

"I definitely remember."

"Good. But now that I think about it, Maverick probably shut that shit down once he found out you was gone. The spot hot now. He too smart to go back," Caleb rationalized.

"You probably right," Shiffon agreed. At this point she was even believing her own lie. "So to warn me about Maverick was the only reason you were trying to get in touch with me?"

"Nah, I was missing you too. After we spent some quality time together at my birthday party, I wanted to follow up wit' some official dates," he smiled.

"That's sweet. We might have to do that."

"Yeah, for sure. But we need to handle this shit. The other reason I reached out to you is because Genesis wants to retain your services again," Caleb revealed.

"Really? What is it this time?"

"That nigga Maverick gotta go. You seem to

be the only person who was able to get next to that nigga."

"Excuse me?!" Caleb's comment had Shiffon about to panic. Her guilty conscious made her paranoid, wondering if her secret was out.

"When you and your crew wiped out Maverick's men at that party and snatched him up." Caleb stated. "I know you ain't forget that shit already."

"Of course not. You have to excuse me. My mind still ain't right after being cooped up in that tiny room for all that time."

"No need to explain. I understand," Caleb reassured Shiffon. "That shit would fuck anybody head up. But yeah, you know how to get at Maverick, so Genesis wants you for the job."

"I don't know if I'm the right person."

"Why not? You got at him once, you can do it again."

"I'm sure he's being extra cautious now, plus I might have another job already lined up."

"Listen, Bad Bitches Only is the best at this assassin shit and yo' other client can wait. Genesis is paying top dollar and if he wants you for the job, then you need to do it," Caleb emphasized.

Shiffon knew Caleb wasn't making a request it was a demand. If she turned the job down, it would only raise suspicion and under the circumstances that was the last thing she needed. So Shiffon did the only thing she could.

"Of course I'll take the job. When would Genesis like for me to start?"

"Like a fuckin' week ago but today will work. This is a priority. I'll make sure you have everything you need. But understand, ain't no kidnapping this time. When you find that nigga, you put two to the dome. We want that muthafucka dead...dead. Understood?"

"Understood." Shiffon grabbed the bottle of wine and was about to take it straight to the head but instead refilled her glass. The pressure she was now under, not even a stiff drink could fix it. Shiffon desperately needed to do the impossible. Devise a plan that would appease Genesis and keep Maverick alive.

"You spoiling me with all these visits!" Skylar lit up when Precious came in her room.

"I guess I'm just happy my friend is back. You know I don't have many of those," Precious laughed.

"Well, you can come visit all you want.

Trust, I love the company. Every time you show up looking like a glam doll, reminds me of all I have to look forward to when I finally get out this damn hospital."

"Girl, you so crazy but I feel you. I've spent a few times laid up in a hospital bed, about to lose my mind," Precious smacked.

"Glad you can sympathize with my dilemma," Skylar smirked.

"Damn sure can," Precious said sitting down, glancing around the room. "I see you got some new fresh flowers since the last time I stopped by," she remarked.

"Yeah, they're from Genesis."

"Oh lawd, them eyes dancing again and it ain't because Genevieve got her daddy back either." Precious shook her head. "You didn't mention anything about having amnesia since waking up from your coma, which means you remember Genesis has a whole wife at home."

"I'm aware Genesis is married to Talisa," Skylar cracked, rolling her eyes.

"Well good. I would hate you confusing Genesis's kindness with him wanting to reunite as a couple."

"Damn, Precious. Is it really necessary for you to kill all my wishful thinking."

"Yes! This is not the time for you to immerse yourself in childhood fairytales."

"Have you ever considered this isn't some figment of my imagination and Genesis actually cares about me?" Skylar declared.

"There is no doubt in my mind Genesis cares about you. As a matter of fact, I believe he loves you and always will. But he's in love with his wife. There's a difference Skylar," Precious explained.

"Then why is he going out his way to be so kind to me? He's come to visit me a few times already. The majority of these flowers are all from Genesis. And when I'm released from the hospital next week, he wants me living at the condo again and is going to make sure I have twenty-four hour security," Skylar boasted with pride. "Clearly his feelings run deep for me."

"I'm not disputing that Skylar. You are the mother of his child and he's protective of you. He's also full of guilt for turning his back on you and Genevieve."

"I'll tell you like I told Genesis. He isn't the blame. How was he supposed to know that Amir was capable of doing something so foul."

"Of course but it doesn't negate the fact Genesis feels guilty. Skylar, you've been given a second chance at life. Don't waste it on chasing after a man who isn't available." Precious hoped telling her friend the truth, would get her mind right. "I know this isn't what you want to hear but Genesis is never leaving Talisa. You deserve to find your own happiness and be with a man who is in love with you and not another woman."

Skylar bowed her head in shame. "You're absolutely right," she hated to admit it but finally did. "Genesis will forever have a piece of my heart but it's time for me to let go and move on. I can't spend the rest of my life carrying a torch for him."

"Can you do that?" Precious asked.

"I have no choice. If only for Genevieve's sake. She deserves to have a close relationship with her father. I'm not going to ruin that by throwing myself at Genesis every chance I get," Skylar laughed nervously. "I can't afford anymore fuckups."

"Girl, I'm proud of you." Precious went over and gave Skylar a hug. "I know it's hard to let go of a man you love with all your heart but trust me, it will get easier. You'll fall in love again," she assured Skylar.

"I hope you're right."

"I know I am. Once you leave this hospital, we'll get you ready to enter the dating scene again. I can even throw you a single lady, I'm coming out party!" Precious laughed.

"You bet not be joking because that's exactly what I need," Skylar beamed.

"Say no more. I'll start planning it now and get the invites ready," Precious said, getting excited.

"I hope you'll have an invite for me too."

Precious and Skylar both turned towards the door to see who had inserted themselves in their conversation.

"Talisa, this is a surprise." Precious tried her best not to gasp. "It's good to see you. It's been awhile." She walked over and gave Talisa a hug.

"Yeah it is a surprise. You're the last person I expected to get a visit from," Skylar admitted.

"I hope you don't mind me coming to visit you," Talisa said, sitting down the flowers she brought. "I see you have more than enough of these," she commented. "There all so beautiful but Genesis has always had exquisite taste."

An awkward silence filled the room. None of the ladies seemed to know how to react after Talisa's comment. They weren't sure if she was being low key shady or simply acknowledging facts.

"Well ladies, I would love to stay and chit

chat but I need to get home and pack," Precious said, grabbing her purse.

"Pack...I didn't know you were going out of town," Skylar frowned.

"Yes but I should only be gone for a couple days. I need to go see Aaliyah," Precious disclosed.

"Is she okay?" Skylar could hear some concern in Precious's voice, although she was trying to do a good job of concealing it.

"She's fine. The moment I get back in town, I'll come visit," Precious promised Skylar, kissing her on the cheek. "Talisa, we have to do lunch. There's tons to catch up on," she smiled, waving bye as she headed to the door.

"That would be great. Call me!" Talisa blew her a kiss before turning her attention back to Skylar once Precious was gone.

"Now that we're alone, why don't you tell me the real reason for your visit. I'm sure it wasn't to bring me flowers," Skylar huffed.

"Do you mind if I sit down?" Talisa asked politely.

"Go right ahead."

"You're looking well."

"Not as well as you," Skylar replied back, staring at the enormous diamond ring on Talisa's wedding finger.

"Skylar, I didn't come here to gloat." Talisa wanted to clarify when she noticed Skylar gazing at her bling.

"If not to rub in my face that Genesis chose you to be his wife and not me, then what?"

"For one, I wanted to see how you were doing."

"You could've saved yourself a trip and directed that question to your husband," Skylar quipped.

"I'd rather speak directly to you. This conversation is long overdue. I felt it was time we spoke woman to woman."

"What is there really left to say, Talisa. You won. You have Genesis."

"I get it. You're hurt because…"

"Just stop!" Skylar shouted, cutting Talisa off. "I don't need you trying to analyze me like you're some therapist. There is no way you can possibly get it because you have the man that you love and I don't and never will. And please don't patronize my feelings by saying I'll meet a man and find love again…blasé blah!" She continued to fuss. "I'll never find another man like Genesis."

"I think it was a mistake for me to come here," Talisa stated, seeing the fury on Skylar's face.

"We finally agree on something." Skylar cut her eyes at Talisa.

"I'll leave but remember one thing, Skylar. You won too. You gave Genesis a beautiful little girl that he absolutely adores. For that reason alone, you'll always have a piece of his heart. My husband will go out of his way to give you whatever you need because you're the mother of his child and there's nothing I can do about it. So although I'm his wife, I still have to share him with you." Talisa expressed her own pain before turning to walk away.

"Talisa, wait!" Skylar called out.

Talisa stopped as she was about to walk out the door. She turned to face the woman she knew was in love with her husband. "What is it?"

"You must think I'm so selfish." Skylar shook her head, trying to fight back the tears. "All this time I was feeling like a victim. That I was about to have this perfect life and you stole it from me. But that's not what happened and I feel so ashamed. You lost all those years with your husband and child because of Arnez. You deserve your happy ending and I'm sorry it took me all this time to realize it," Skylar sobbed. "I hope one day you can forgive me."

"No forgiveness necessary," Talisa said, walking over and wrapping her arms around Skylar. The two women embraced, releasing all the resentment they had for each other.

"That was so hard for me to say. Thank you for making it a lot easier." Skylar said nervously.

"It wasn't my intention but I'm glad I did," Talisa smiled sweetly. "I know we might never be besties but I do hope this is the beginning of a possible friendship."

"I would like that, if only for Genevieve's benefit. You are her father's wife and I know in a lot of ways she'll also see you as her mother too."

"Will you be okay with that?" Talisa asked.

"The question is are you?" Skylar wanted to know.

"Yes! I would never try and replace you as her mother but I will love and protect Genevieve as if she was my own. I can promise you that," Talisa assured her.

"Thank you. My daughter is a very lucky little girl. She'll grow up surrounded by love."

"Yes she will." Skylar and Talisa once again embraced. Their mutual love for Genesis and Genevieve allowed them to finally find a common ground. The women were able to put the past behind them and get along, in order to do what was in the best interest of the child.

Chapter Six

In My Feelings

"You sure that's her?" Micah asked Cam as they watched Celinda playing with her daughter at the park.

"Positive. You see the car parked over there," Cam pointed to the black sapphire Escalade. "That's Prevan's truck. It was a gift from his brother Caleb when he got outta jail. The nigga be letitn' his baby mama hold it."

"You sure we can get her to crack?" Micah wanted to know before they wasted their time.

"Yeah, I heard she a real grimy bitch. Always

plottin' on a nigga wit' some money. Ain't got no loyalty. She the reason her man got locked up the first time."

"And he still fuckin' wit' the hoe," Micah shook his head. "The nigga didn't learn you can't get yo' feelings wrapped up in a snake bitch."

"He ain't learned yet but he about to," Cam nodded. "Go head and pull up."

"Come on, Amelia. It's time to meet daddy," Celinda said, holding her daughter's hand. As they were walking towards the Escalade, she got sidetracked when she noticed the alpine white Range Rover Autobiography slowly turning the corner. She was ready to salivate, thinking about how much the ride cost.

"Excuse me Ma, you married?" Cam rolled down the window and asked Celinda.

"Nah, I'm not married yet. Why you lookin' for a wife?" Celinda teased.

"Might be, you interested?" Cam flirted back.

"It depends."

"On what?"

"Mommy, we have to go. Daddy is waiting for us." Amelia tugged at her mother's hand.

"Hold on a minute," Celinda said to Cam.

"Take yo' time, Ma."

"Baby, mommy has to talk to this man for

one second. He's a friend of daddy's," Celinda told her daughter, putting Amelia in her car seat before walking over to Cam. "Sorry about that."

"No problem. I understand you gotta take care of yo' little one. So when you gonna let me take you out?" Cam asked, playing with Celinda's hair.

"Where you takin' me?"

"Anywhere you want."

"I need to do some shopping."

"We can do that. It's all on me. Whatever you want." Cam was telling Celinda everything she wanted to hear. She gave up those digits without hesitation. "I'ma call you later on."

"I'll be waiting," she smiled, waving goodbye.

"I'ma have fun turning that bitch out," Cam laughed.

"I'm sure you will. Just make sure you wrap up. Ain't no tellin' where that pussy been," Micah warned before they drove off.

"I know you dealing with a lot of business in Philly, so I appreciate you coming to New York on such short notice," Genesis said to Caleb when he arrived at his office.

"No problem, boss. You already know, I'm always available for you." Caleb stated, sitting down in the chair across from Genesis's desk. "So what you need?"

"Last time we talked, you said you were trying to make contact with Shiffon. Where you at with that?" Genesis inquired.

"I was able to sit down with her the other day and she's onboard."

"Good. Did you tell her to get to work asap?"

"Yep. I told her killin' Maverick is top priority. Shiffon understands you need this done immediately," Caleb made clear, stretching out his legs, getting comfortable in the chair.

"That's an accurate statement. Maverick is turning into Arnez 2.0. so I need that nigga dealt with."

"Has something else happened? You seem concerned."

"There's been no movement from him since everything went down in the Bronx. That makes me uneasy. There's always quiet before the storm, which means Maverick is somewhere plotting his next move. We need to strike first," Genesis said wearily.

"Shiffon and her crew got him once before, they'll get him again." Caleb was confident with his choice of words.

"I want you to be right. But to better the odds, I put this cat named Bloodhound, another hired gun I've used in the past on it. He's tryna track Maverick's whereabouts now. He's ruthless and fearless. So between him and Shiffon's crew, one of them should be able to get the job done. At least that's what I'm hoping, cause I can't take much more bad," Genesis admitted.

"Speaking of bad, is Nico making any progress?"

"As of yet, no." Genesis balled up the paper he was writing something down on and tossed it in the trash, as if he was trying to relieve his stress.

"Sorry to hear that. Nico seems like good people. I'm praying he pulls through."

"Me too." Genesis said gravely. "If Nico's doctor doesn't see improvement soon then he's..." Genesis's voice faded off. He wouldn't allow himself to say what seemed like the inevitable. "We need to focus on getting rid of Maverick," he said, switching topics.

"Shiffon is on it," Caleb reiterated. "I don't want you to worry."

"I'll stop worrying once I can dig Maverick's grave. But while I'm waiting on that, business can't stop. Understandably... everyone is preoccupied at the moment, so I need you to step in and handle some business here in New York for me," Genesis announced. "I know you call Philly home and your family is there. Will this be a problem?"

"Hell no! It'll be an honor stepping up and handling business on your behalf. Just tell me what I need to do boss," Caleb stated with a proud grin on his face.

The more Genesis got to know Caleb and spend time with him, the more the ambitious young man reminded him of himself. His eyes were heavy with hunger, to the point his unyielding determination made him lack fear. He was everything Genesis wanted and needed for his successor. The problem was Caleb wasn't his son, although he wanted him to be.

I shouldn't have come back. I should've stayed away. This is the last time we're having sex then I'm done... Shiffon thought to herself as her nails pressed into Maverick's back while he thrusted deeper inside her. If this was really going to be the last time, then Shiffon would have no worries about her sexual escapades with Maverick. The problem was, she had told herself this very same thing a few days ago but yet here Shiffon was back again for the third time. He had awaken the erotic desires she'd buried away. If it was any other man, Shiffon would've thought of their sexual encounters as a much needed stress reliever. But Maverick wasn't any man. He should be dead right now but instead he had Shiffon feeling very much alive.

"We have to stop doing this." Shiffon laid on her back, breathing heavily after having her second orgasm.

"Why would you wanna stop a good thing." Maverick gave Shiffon a wicked smile before kissing her hardened nipple.

"Stop it!" She giggled, playfully pushing Maverick's head away. "We're not about to do this again...I'm exhausted. No more sex!" Shiffon protested.

"Fine. You can relax while I run out for a minute. But when I get back, you can't deny me," Maverick said, leaning in for a kiss.

"There you go giving me that look."

"What look?" he asked getting out of the bed.

"You know what look I'm talking about. That stare you give me."

"Oh, that stare like I'm making love to you with my eyes." Maverick stated knowingly.

"You ain't shit." Shiffon laughed, shaking her head. "So you just leaving me here."

"I would let you come wit' me but I know we keeping this relationship on the low low," Maverick said putting on his clothes. "So we can't take no chances of being seen together," he continued.

"True. But why do you have to go now? Can't you wait until after I go back to my hotel room?" Shiffon questioned.

"For one, I don't want you to leave. I was hoping you'd stay the night. Two, I have to meet Fatima and give her this money before their flight leave in the morning."

"So you leaving me to give the next chick some money?"

"Fatima is family. She's the mother of my Godson. Who in a lot of ways is like my son now, since his father is no longer with us," Maverick added.

"I'm sorry to hear that. What happened to his father?"

"You killed him. My fault, one of the other chicks who was workin' that party wit' you killed my man Klay. That nigga was like a brother to me."

"I wasn't expecting you to say that." Shiffon put her head down. "Damn, that shit cut deep," she sighed.

"That wasn't my intention. You asked me a question and I answered it. But I told you before. I don't blame you for what happened to my crew. Genesis is responsible. I get he wanted to save his daughter but what about Klay's son. He has to grow up without a father. That's why the nigga gotta be dealt wit'." Maverick once again stressed his intentions to bring down Genesis. The man he blamed for eliminating the people closest to him.

"You have to know it wasn't Genesis's intention to rob a little boy of his father."

"Why are you so fuckin' stuck on defending that man?" Maverick scoffed. "It ain't enough that I don't blame you. You want me to forgive that nigga too. Why?!"

"Because I don't wanna lose you!" Shiffon yelled. Hating to admit her truth.

"Who said you had to. I'm not puttin' you in the middle of this shit. As a matter of fact, we don't even have to discuss it. Your dealings wit' Genesis is done and so you not feeling some kinda way, whatever moves I make, I won't share wit' you. It allows you to stay neutral. You don't need to know anyway. Now, I'll see you when I get back," Maverick said, leaving out the room.

Maverick believed he had it all figured out but Shiffon knew the truth. Her dealings with Genesis were far from done. He hired her to finish the job no one had been able to do. But she caught major feelings for dude. Not only that, Maverick had allowed her to live, when he could've easily let her die. Shiffon was now torn because not only did she care about him, she also felt she owed Maverick for sparing her life.

Chapter Seven

In The Midst Of Darkness

It was a stormy summer night. You could hear the whistling wind and rain thrusting against the windowsill. Genesis and Talisa were wrapped in each other's arms sleeping peacefully. It was the calm before the storm. It started with Genesis's cell phone ringing nonstop. Once that went unanswered the home phone started ringing, which was rare. So rare, it immediately woke Genesis up from his sleep.

"Hello," he answered, still in a partial daze.

"Is everything okay?" Talisa mumbled, when she no longer felt the warmth of her husband's arms. But she got no response from Genesis. With the moonlight peeping through the massive windows, she could clearly see the expression on her husband's face. It was consumed with dread.

"I have to go." Genesis finally said.

"Baby, what's wrong? What happened?" Talisa questioned, following after her husband when he got out of bed. But once again Genesis went silent. Shock had left him at a loss for words. He didn't want to believe he had awaken to a nightmare.

"Who knew Mission Hills, Kansas would have such an exquisite hotel," Precious commented to Amir as they sat in the lobby. She marveled at the hand-blown Venetian glass chandeliers floating overhead. Admiring the intricately carved wood paneling and lively Renaissance artwork adorning the walls.

"That sounds like something Aaliyah would say," Amir smiled.

"Well, she is my daughter," Precious remarked as her eyes continued to scan the lobby.

"Speaking of your daughter, look who just walked in," Amir said, nudging her arm. Precious jumped up so quick, Amir barely had time to put down his drink, so he could catch up to her.

"Aaliyah, are you okay...what happened to your head?" she questioned, placing her hand on the bandage.

"I'm fine, Mother! What are you and Amir doing here?"

"First, tell me about your head."

"Oh, this," Aaliyah touched the bandage. "It's nothing. I slipped and fell. Now do you want to tell me what brings you all the way to Kansas?"

"You know why we're here," Amir stated. "Don't make this difficult, Aaliyah."

"Is it because I turned my phone off? I mean, I simply wanted some time alone to relax. I apologize for worrying both of you. But as you can see, I'm fine. You can head to the airport and get back to New York." Aaliyah gave her mother and Amir a brief hug. "I'll walk you out."

"Aaliyah, it's over. Cut the shit," Precious popped. "We came here to get Justina's baby and we're not leaving until we get him."

"You sound crazy. I don't know what you're

talking about. I don't have Justina's baby!" Aaliyah adamantly denied.

"Fine," Precious shrugged, taking her phone out her purse.

"What are doing?" Aaliyah questioned.

"Calling the police. I think they should know that a child who has been reported missing in Miami, Florida, is right here in this upscale hotel."

"You wouldn't dare!" Aaliyah snapped, reaching to grab the phone out of her mother's hand.

"Oh, yes the hell I will. If it's the only way to put an end to this foolishness, then so be it. You're not leaving me much of a choice, Aaliyah."

"Yes I am. You and Amir can turn around and leave this hotel and pretend this conversation never happened."

"Aaliyah, come on, don't do this. You don't kidnap babies...you're better than that." Amir tried reasoning with her.

"This coming from the guy who took a baby away from her father, by doing so, put his own sister at risk because you decided to pay someone to switch a DNA test."

"You told her about that?" Amir frowned at Precious.

"Yes she did, so stop acting like you're some saint," Aaliyah snarled at Amir. "Both of you.

Mother, you have plenty of skeletons of your own too!"

"Our skeletons change nothing, Aaliyah. Maya kidnapped you, when you were a baby, which you're well aware of. That was the scariest time of my life. I will not allow you to continue to do this to another woman."

"Justina doesn't deserve that beautiful, sweet baby upstairs!" Aaliyah belted.

"You can't play God. It isn't your decision to make."

"What about me and my baby?" she questioned. "Why did God give Justina the perfect child and deny me mine," Aaliyah wept, collapsing in her mother's arms. "It isn't fair. It just isn't fair."

"I know, my sweet baby girl, I know. But it's time to bring Justina's baby back home." Precious stroked Aaliyah's hair, allowing her daughter to let it all out. All the pain, anger and sadness she was still holding on to. Instead of healing for the past few months, Aaliyah had been harboring her agony but now she had to let it go.

Genesis wanted to believe he was still stuck in a bad dream not wanting to admit this was his reality. But he could no longer deny the truth when he entered the hospital.

"She's gone! My baby is gone!" Skylar's mom cried as Genesis held her in his arms.

"I can't believe she's no longer here." Genesis was holding Skylar's mom tightly in disbelief. "I thought Skylar had made a full recovery and was coming home soon."

"She was."

"So what happened...why did she take a turn for the worse?" Genesis needed clarification. "And why are there police officers here?" he asked, noticing them coming out of Skylar's room.

"Skylar was murdered, Genesis. Somebody killed my baby," she bawled.

"What?!" In shock, Genesis abruptly stepped back. He placed his hands firmly on her arms as they locked eyes. "What did you just say?"

"Skylar was murdered! A monster came in this hospital and murdered my baby!" She yelled, tears streaming down her face.

"No! What about the security I had posted in front of her room."

"They found him in the bathroom dead. You couldn't protect her. My granddaughter lost her mother and I lost my only child," she sobbed.

Genesis felt like shit. Watching Skylar's

mother breakdown right in front of his eyes was too much for him. *I failed her, Skylar and my daughter. Genevieve will grow up without her mother and I'll never forgive myself,* Genesis thought to himself walking off to make a phone call.

"Man, it's the middle of the fuckin' night. Whatever you calling about can't be good," Supreme mumbled when he answered the phone.

"I need you to double up security on Nico. Somebody has to be at his side every fuckin' second. We have to get on top of this shit right now!" Genesis seethed.

"Yo, what the fuck happened?" Supreme rose up in bed, now wide awake. "Genesis, talk to me!" He shouted, detecting the urgency in his voice.

Genesis was having a hard time saying the words out loud. He knew once he did, it meant it was true. "It's Skylar," he finally said.

"What about Skylar...is she okay?" Supreme asked with concern.

"No, she's not okay. Skylar's dead." His voice cracked and part of Genesis's heart was broken.

"Are you serious...not Skylar. Amir told me the other day she was about to be released from the hospital."

"She was but I gotta call in the middle of the

night and came to the hospital. When I got here, I found out she was murdered. So was the security detail I hired to watch over her."

"Damn, Genesis. Man, I'm so sorry to hear about Skylar. I know how much you cared about her. That shit fucked up and my guess is, Maverick behind this," Supreme stated with certainty.

"Of course it was that muthafucker!" Genesis was foaming at the mouth. "We have to make sure Nico and everyone we love is protected. Ain't no tellin' what that niggas next move gonna be."

"I know you put that nigga Bloodhound on it. He ain't making no progress?" Supreme inquired.

"Last time I spoke to him, he had a couple leads but nothing concrete. He need to track that muthafucka down soon. Until then, we just have to keep our people safe."

"I'll take care of Nico, you handle things on yo' end. Keep me in the loop and watch over Precious until I come home." Supreme told him.

"No doubt. I'll be in touch soon," Genesis said, ending his call with Supreme. He walked back over to Skylar's mother and held her, trying to comfort her as best he could.

Chapter Eight

Die For Me

"Yes Papi! You fuck me so good!" Celinda scre-amed out as Cam had her bent over on the living room couch dicking her down. He was slapping her ass, pulling her hair and she ate that shit up. Their fuck sessions were much different than the ones she shared with her baby daddy and Celinda loved every second of it.

Between the rough sex, expensive dinners and a few shopping sprees, Cam had Celinda completely open. To the point she had started scheming on how to get him to fuck her raw, so she could get pregnant and make him baby daddy number 2. But Cam had another agenda. And he was now ready to implement his plan.

"Damn baby, you got some good pussy," Cam said, after they were done fucking.

"This pussy would feel even better if you take that condom off," Celinda smiled, leaning over to kiss Cam.

"I bet it would but a nigga might get all caught up and forget to pull out," he joked.

"I wouldn't care."

"Yeah but I bet yo' baby father would."

"Maybe I want another baby daddy. We'd make a pretty baby together. We can start right now." Celinda bit down on her bottom lip.

"Is that right?" Cam pretended to be interested in her proposition.

"Yep." Celinda crawled over to Cam who had put his jeans back on and was sitting on the couch. She unzipped them, pulling down his briefs, letting her tongue dance on his dick.

"Damn, you ain't lettin' up on a nigga," Cam moaned, as his dick instantly got back hard when Celinda put her wet mouth around the tip. He leaned back, enjoying her deep throating skills.

While Celinda believed all the fucking and sucking she'd been giving Cam was getting her closer to locking him down to be her man. He on the other hand knew it meant Celinda was ready to be put to work.

Shiffon woke up to soft kisses being sprinkled on her shoulders. "I'm really starting to get used to this," she smiled.

"Then my plan is working," Maverick said, lifting Shiffon's hair and kissing the back of her neck.

"What plan is that?"

"To keep you all to myself."

"Whatever!" Shiffon giggled, turning around in the bed, locking lips with Maverick. The two were about to make love but Maverick's burner phone started ringing.

"Babe, I've been waiting for this call. I gotta take this," Maverick said kissing Shiffon one more time before getting out of the bed. "Yo," Maverick answered, exiting the bedroom.

Shiffon couldn't help but smile as she watched Maverick leave. She knew they shared an undeniable chemistry from the moment they met at that party but never did she think he would make her feel like this. As Shiffon began to get lost in her thoughts, her own phone started to ring. It was Caleb. At first she wasn't going to answer but he called back again.

"Hello." Shiffon tried to keep her voice down.

"You sleep?" Caleb asked.

"Sorta, what's going on?"

"Maverick got shit fucked up out here."

"Did something else happen?" the tone in Caleb's voice had Shiffon's heart racing. It wasn't filled with his usual anger and contempt. There was a sense of anguish and distress.

"Skylar, the mother of Genesis's daughter is dead."

"You talking about the woman that Arnez nigga kidnapped. I thought she had made a full recovery?"

"Yeah she did. But that cold blooded mut-hafucka Maverick had his people go to her hospital room and murder her." Caleb's rage echoed through the phone.

Shiffon swallowed hard. She felt like she needed to gasp for air. "Are you sure Maverick was behind the murder?"

"Who the fuck else would it be?! Of course it was Maverick. He had the killer put a fuckin' bullet through her head. Skylar can't even have an open casket. Now where you at on trackin' that nigga down? Genesis is willing to pay you double."

"Caleb, slow down. This isn't about the money," Shiffon said as her voice cracked.

"What else would it fuckin' be about when it comes to hiring you for yo' services?" Caleb wanted to know.

"All the money in the world can't make me find a mark who doesn't want to be found," Shiffon explained.

"Well the bigger the price tag on the mark should motivate you to track him the fuck down!" Caleb shot back.

"You're right, it does give me more resources to try and locate him. I'm doing all that I can."

"You need to do more. We need that nigga found before he do anymore damage. So get that shit done, Shiffon!" Caleb barked.

"I'm on it. I'll be in touch soon," Shiffon promised, quickly ending the call when she heard the bedroom door opening.

"Who were you on the phone with?" Maverick asked when he came back in the bedroom.

"I should be asking you the same question."

"I asked you first," Maverick laughed.

"This isn't funny!" Shiffon snapped.

"Yo hold up. Maybe I stepped in the wrong

room. What happened to the beautiful, sweet woman I left waiting for me in the bed?" Maverick smiled.

"Please tell me you are not the reason an innocent little baby no longer has her mother."

The smile immediately vanished from Maverick's face. "I told you we weren't gonna do this."

"No! Whatever this is, we didn't discuss. Because if we had, I would've begged you not to have that woman murdered. Skylar had nothing to do with this. Nothing!" Shiffon cried.

"The call you were just on, was it Genesis... oh of course not, he don't speak to the hired help. So who was it? Let me guess...Caleb."

"Why does it matter?"

"Just answer the question. I know the nigga gotta hard on for you. He was probably dying for a reason to whine on the phone and of course you took the call."

"Caleb doesn't have a hard on for me!" Shiffon became defensive.

"I saw you with him at his birthday party. That nigga had his hands all over you."

"You were at Caleb's birthday party? I didn't see you there." Shiffon said nervously.

"That was the point. Are you fuckin' that

nigga?" Maverick grabbed Shiffon by her jaw and lifted her face up. "Answer the fuckin' question," he cursed.

"No! I'm not fuckin' Caleb!" She protested.

"You betta not be." He threatened, releasing her from his grasp.

"Maverick, do you know what you've done?"

"Yeah. I did what the fuck I was supposed to do and I'm far from finished. I told you to stay outta this shit and you shoulda listened," he warned.

"I can't stay out of it!" Shiffon yelled.

"Why the fuck not?! If you ain't fuckin' the nigga why you care how I handle this shit?" Maverick pressed but Shiffon said nothing. She just gave him this blank stare. "Oh, I get it. You back on the payroll."

"It's not…"

"Don't deny the shit. How long you been back workin' for Genesis?"

"I don't work for Genesis."

"Don't spin this shit. You supposed to kill me. So what happened?"

Shiffon put her head down. "I don't wanna have this conversation."

"What's the problem? You supposed to be an assassin…that's what you do right?" Maverick taunted. "I'll make it easy for you." He reached in the top drawer of the nightstand next to the bed. "Here take it," he said, tossing the gun to Shiffon. "It's loaded. All you have to do is pull the trigger."

"Why are you doing this?" Shiffon pushed the gun away.

"You know why. You been layin' up in the bed wit' me. Fuckin' me...tongue down my throat and plottin' to kill me the whole time."

"It wasn't like that."

"Then how was it? I need you to explain that shit to me. How can you be planning on murdering me while suckin' my dick at the same time?!" Maverick mocked.

"You actin' like I want you to die! I never planned on killing you!" Shiffon screamed out in frustration.

"Then why did you take the fuckin' job?!" he roared.

"I didn't have a choice!"

"You always have a fuckin' choice." Maverick continued to curse as he voice reverberated through the room. He grabbed the gun and placed it in Shiffon's hand. "Now go ahead and finish the job you got hired to do," he stated, pressing the barrel of the gun to his chest. Daring Shiffon to pull the trigger.

Chapter Nine

Have Faith

"How's Aaliyah doing?" Amir asked Precious when she came back downstairs.

"She's resting. Playing all that hide and seek, has drained her, mentally and physically. Sleep is what she needs. How's the little one?" Precious smiled, kissing Desi's hand. "He really is a beautiful baby."

"Yeah, he is. I know Justina must miss him something terrible," Amir said, cradling the little boy in his arms. "And no I'm not defending Aaliyah but I get this is hard for her too."

"I'm sure but it's time to make this right, so don't get too attached because baby Desi is going home to his family tomorrow," Precious reminded Amir. "I would take him home this evening but attending the gathering Genesis is having for Skylar is all I can emotionally deal with today."

"I understand. All I was trying to say was, I get why it was difficult for Aaliyah to let Desi go. I never understood when I would hear people say, babies are a blessing. I get it now. When you hold them, you feel healed."

"Very true. If only they could stay little and sweet like this forever," Precious laughed. "But you're right. This is going to be extremely hard on Aaliyah. It's going to take all of our support to get her through it. I pray to God, Supreme, Nico and Lorenzo come back to us soon because Aaliyah will need both of her father's more than ever."

"I agree. How do you think T-Roc is going to react when you bring him Desi tomorrow?"

"Hopefully, he'll be so grateful to have his grandson back, he won't go ballistic on me."

"I think it would be a good idea if you let me come with you," Amir advised. "He's very close to my father and we have a pretty decent relationship too. I can be like a buffer."

"Oh goodness, you make me feel like I need to show up strapped," Precious sighed.

"I'm not saying T-Roc is gonna try to kill you but your daughter did have his daughter's baby kidnapped. It's a given, the tension is gonna be extra thick."

"I get it. I wanted you to stay with Aaliyah but I think she'll be okay by herself for a couple hours. Tomorrow when we go into the city, we'll drop Aaliyah off at her place first, then we'll take Desi to T-Roc. He can make the necessary arrangements to get the baby back to Justina in Miami."

"Do you think there's a chance Justina is still in Kansas? She did track Aaliyah down and got into that fight with her."

"I'm sure after she was released from jail, her next stop was back to the hotel. Once Justina found out Aaliyah checked out, I'm positive she couldn't leave Kansas fast enough. And she has no idea where Aaliyah went because we used the private jet to get home. Justina is probably back in Miami with her husband deciding if she wants to have my daughter thrown in jail for felony kidnapping, or if it would be more gratifying to execute her own form of justice."

"I am surprised Justina hasn't gone to the

police yet. Having Aaliyah do years behind bars for kidnapping, would be the ultimate revenge."

"I have no idea what Justina is thinking. The important thing is, we have her son and he's safe. I believe that trumps everything else. Plus, Aaliyah unfairly spent all that time in jail because of Chantal and partially because of Justina. T-Roc is a businessman and a father. I'm sure with your help, we can convince him to agree, the slate has now been wiped clean and we can call it even," Precious rationalized.

"If you say so."

"Thanks for being so optimistic," Precious remarked sarcastically. "I have to get ready to go. I'm already running late," she said grabbing her purse.

"I wish I could go with you. Please pay my respects to Skylar's family. I'm having a hard time believing she's gone," Amir admitted somberly.

"It's best you respect your father's wishes," Precious emphasized. "No one has forgotten the stunt you pulled Amir, especially not Genesis."

"I know and I get why he doesn't want me there but..."

"But nothing," Precious said, cutting Amir off. 'This day is about the people who loved Skylar, coming together to remember what a wonderful mother, daughter and friend she was. So stop your whining Amir. Now do you wanna walk out with me?"

"No, I think I'll stay here for a little while longer and keep baby Desi company," Amir smiled, staring into the little boy's eyes.

"Fine. Just make sure you let Maria know when you're about to leave, so she can tend to Desi. I want Aaliyah having as little contact with him as possible. We don't need her to relapse," Precious stressed.

"No worries. Desi is in good hands with me. I'll see you tomorrow," he said, giving a slight wave bye to Precious. "We need to get this little guy back home to his mother as soon as possible." Amir continued to stare deeply into Desi's eyes, completely enthralled with the beautiful baby boy.

"Precious, thank you for coming," Genesis said giving her a hug.

"I'm sorry I couldn't make the funeral but I was out of town dealing with some issues with Aaliyah," she explained. *Issues is an understatement* Precious thought to herself, not wanting to unload her burdens on Genesis. "But Aaliyah sends her condolences."

"I understand. This was all so unexpected. I'm just glad you were able to join us."

"Of course. You know how much I loved Skylar. I still can't believe she's gone," Precious conceded, wiping away a single tear. "This gathering you're having in her honor is beautiful though. That picture of her is so lovely," she said staring at the large black and white photo next to the 8 feet high and 6 feet wide easel floral arrangement.

"I wanted everything to be just right. The way she would've liked," Genesis said solemnly.

"It's perfect. Skylar would be proud." Precious stroked his arm. She could see the pain in his eyes. "Genesis, in time it will get easier. You know I'm here for you and for Genevieve. Where is my beautiful Goddaughter?"

"I actually just put her down for a nap."

"If you don't mind, I would love to just peep in on her. See her face. I promise not to wake her."

"Of course. You know where her bedroom is. A few more of Skylar's relatives just walked in. I'ma go speak to them while you check on Genevieve," Genesis said, kissing Precious on the cheek before walking away.

Precious made small talk with a few people as she headed to Genevieve's bedroom. When she got there, she saw Talisa standing over the crib. "She's such a beautiful baby," Precious said in a low tone.

"Precious, you startled me. I didn't hear you come in," Talisa whispered.

"I didn't want to wake Genevieve. Nothing is sweeter than a sleeping baby. They look so angelic," Precious smiled. "Then they wake up," she joked.

"I know what you mean. I find myself constantly staring at Genevieve while she sleeps. I guess in a way, I'm trying to make up for all those times I never got to see Amir sleeping when he was a baby."

"Having that time stolen away from you is unforgivable."

"It is." Talisa shook her head thinking of all the years she was robbed of. "But I refuse to allow Arnez to steal away any more of my joy."

"That's wise. I wish I could be as rational thinking as you," Precious remarked.

"Can I ask you a question?"

"Of course."

"I know how close you were to Skylar, so do

you promise not to be offended by my question?" Talisa wanted to know.

"At this point in my life it takes a lot to offend me. So yes, I promise."

"Does it make me a horrible person that I feel blessed to be able to raise Skylar's baby? I hate it happened under these tragic circumstances but I truly do love Genevieve like she's my very own daughter."

"No it doesn't make you a horrible person. I had a chance to speak with Skylar before she was killed. She told me the two of you had a heart to heart and were finally in a good place. I know she's smiling down and giving you her blessing. There is no one better to raise her daughter than you."

"Thank you so much for saying that, Precious." Talisa reached over and gave her a huge hug.

"It's the truth but don't forget, I'm still the Godmother and always available for babysitting duties," Precious smiled.

"I will hold you to it," Talisa beamed as the women continued to embrace. Together they mourned Skylar but relished at the idea of making her proud by raising her daughter to be absolutely amazing.

"Amir, what are you doing here? Shouldn't you be at the service Genesis is having for Skylar?" Supreme asked when he let him in his hotel suite.

"My father didn't want me there. I can't say that I blame him," Amir said, sitting down on one of the plush sofas. After Amir left Precious's estate, he had a lot on his mind. The only person he felt he could have an honest conversation with was Supreme.

"Genesis is taking Skylar's murder hard, which is to be expected. He also blames himself for what happened to her."

"And he blames me. If only I had never changed that paternity test. Things would be so different right now," Amir reasoned.

"Maybe or maybe not. But you can't speculate on what's already happened. You'll drive yourself crazy. Did you fuck up… yes but we've all fucked up. Unfortunately for you, you never had the chance to make things right with Skylar before she died. Luckily you will have the opportunity to do right by Skylar's daughter and your little sister," Supreme said patting Amir on the shoulder.

"What about my dad. Is he ever gonna forgive me or blame me for the rest of my life?"

"Honestly, I don't know. Genesis can be a forgiving man but also a stubborn one. We all seem to have that same trait. You just have to give your father time."

"I know you're right but it's hard. When he told me not to show up, it was like a stab to the heart. I thought we were making strides but now that Skylar's gone, it's like he's shutting me out again," Amir sighed.

"Listen, I'm not gonna judge you because I'm guilty of the same shit."

"What you did and what I did aren't really the same. Precious was your wife when she got pregnant with Aaliyah. Not only that, Nico did kill your unborn child. You had justifiable reasons."

"True but it was still wrong. Luckily Nico and Aaliyah were able to have a close relationship. But I did have to deal with the consequences of my actions and that's the point I'm trying to make to you. You fucked up and you have to man up, which means dealing with the fallout. Eventually, Genesis will forgive you but you can't rush it. It has to be on his time, not yours," Supreme stated.

"You right. I have to keep reminding myself

of that. In the meantime do everything possible to make him proud."

"Now you manning up," Supreme clapped his hands together. "We got that out the way, tell me more about you and Precious trip to Kansas. You really haven't given me any details."

"I think I should let Precious tell you exactly what happened."

Supreme raised an eyebrow. "I know it had something to do with Aaliyah. Is she in some kind of trouble? If so you need to speak up now or Genesis won't be the only person you have a problem with."

"Supreme, you know I have the utmost respect for you but I think this is a conversation you should have with your wife. I will say Aaliyah is doing a lot better. Precious almost has everything under control."

"What do you mean almost?" Supreme got up from his chair and stood over Amir who appeared extremely uncomfortable.

"As you know we just got back in town and Precious wanted to attend the gathering my dad is having for Skylar..."

"Get to the point, Amir!" Supreme barked.

"So tomorrow I'm linking up with Precious and we're going to finish handling everything...

hopefully." Amir mumbled the last word under his breath.

"What are you not telling me?" Supreme demanded to know.

"Man, please just trust me but most importantly trust your wife. I have to believe Precious will get this handled. Have faith," Amir smiled, praying he was right.

Chapter Ten

Bad Blood

"What happened to you taking me to get a new car yesterday," Celinda snapped at Prevan while he was watching Snowfall.

"Don't worry about the car. I got you," he said wanting to get back to watching his show.

"You got me...when, Prevan?! I need an exact fuckin' date!" She huffed folding her arms. When he didn't answer, Celinda stood in front of the television.

"Yo would you move! You makin' me miss some important shit!"

"What's more important than the mother of yo' child having a nice car to drive?"

"You do have a nice car! You always drivin' my shit anyway," Prevan shrugged.

"A 2016 Maxima ain't no nice car," Celinda complained. "That's why I'm always driving yo' Escalade."

"Man, a Maxima is nice and that shit fully loaded too." Prevan shook his head.

"If it's so fuckin' nice, why don't you drive it! Now I'ma ask you again, when we gonna go get my new whip?"

"Caleb is out of town. I'm waiting for Floyd to bring me over some product. He was supposed to come the other day but got held up. He promised to come tonight. Once I get rid of it, I'll have more than enough to get yo' car," Prevan explained.

"Why the fuck you gotta wait on Floyd? You ain't got access to that shit yo'self? You Caleb's brother and he got you workin' for his friend!" Celinda popped, steady stirring the pot.

"Listen, I don't work for Floyd, we all work for Caleb. That's who I answer to."

"Then why the fuck you gotta wait on Floyd to supply you. You don't know where Caleb keep his drugs?"

"Of course I fuckin' know!" Prevan barked,

getting riled up.

"No the fuck you don't!" Celinda shot back, purposely pushing his buttons.

"Yes the fuck. I do!"

"Then where...where Caleb keep his drugs?"

"This spot over on E Dunton St."

"Then why don't you take yo' ass over there and get some product then?"

"Man, stop worrying 'bout how shit get handled. I told you Floyd bringin' what I need tonight. He should be here any minute. So chill the fuck out! You gon' get yo' car. Now can you move, so I can watch my fuckin' show," Prevan fumed.

"A'ight but I betta have some new wheels this time next week or we gon' have a problem," Celinda threatened before storming off into the kitchen.

A few minutes later just as Prevan predicted, Floyd showed up with his goodies. Celinda made sure to ear hustle on their conversation, hoping to overhear some useful information.

"Man, this was all I could bring you," Floyd said, handing Prevan a small duffel bag. "It should be enough to hold you over."

"Hold me over until when?" Prevan questioned, unzipping the bag.

"Caleb is still in New York. He got held up for a few more days. But when I spoke to him earlier today, he said a new shipment will be delivered to the warehouse over on Dunton next Friday."

"Okay cool but is he gon' be back in time for Amelia's birthday party this weekend?"

"Of course! You know that nigga ain't gonna miss his niece's birthday."

"You gon' be there too, right?" Prevan asked.

"No doubt! We fam. Where else I'ma be. Already got her gift," Floyd grinned. "Now let me go. Got my lil shorty waitin' in the car."

Celinda had been taking mental notes while listening to Floyd and Prevan's conversation. Once she felt satisfied with what she heard, her next move was to text Cam with the info. Celinda figured if all went as planned, she wouldn't need Prevan to buy her a new car, she would be able to get it herself.

"Are you sure this is the ideal way to handle such a disturbing situation?" Amir asked Precious as he parked the car.

"Disturbing?" Precious rolled her eyes at Amir.

"I couldn't think of a better word to describe what we're dealing with without possibly offending you," he shrugged.

"I'm sure we can both agree there is nothing ideal about this. Trust me, if there was an easier way, I'd jump on it. But the options are limited to fucked or severely fucked," Precious sighed, taking a moment to think about exactly what she was going to say before proceeding.

Precious rarely let her nerves get the best of her but she would need to humble herself, if she had any chance of making this right. She closed her eyes and exhaled.

"Are you gonna knock or should I?" Amir questioned, wondering if her anxiety was finally kicking in and Precious was having second thoughts. She glanced over at Amir and rang the doorbell. When T-Roc opened the door, to his astonishment, there stood Amir and Precious, who was holding his grandson.

"This is a first. T-Roc is speechless." Precious gave him a pleasant smile. "We come in peace. Bringing you and your family the greatest gift you could ever possibly want," she said, placing the baby in T-Roc's arms. Desi made a high pitched squealing noise, the sound he made when delighted.

"T-Roc, is that a baby I hear?" Chantal asked, coming down the stairs. She stopped when she reached the bottom of the staircase, putting her hand across her chest. For a second, Amir and Precious were scared she was on the verge of having a heart attack. "Dear God, is that my grandson?"

"Yes, it is?" Amir answered the question, since T-Roc remained mute. This was the very first time Chantal or T-Roc had seen their grandchild in person.

"Please, let me hold him," Chantal said, to her husband.

"Not yet," T-Roc spoke up and said. "This is my first time holding my grandson. Just give me a minute." He walked to the living room and sat down in his favorite chair near the fireplace. In the wintertime, T-Roc would sit there with the fire burning, drink a glass of cognac while listening to old school classics. He now envisioned having his grandson right by his side during those times. Chantal joined her husband in the living room while Precious and Amir lingered in the back, giving them their moment.

"In a perfect world, they would remain completely in awe of their grandson, to the point it would eliminate all the hatred, I'm sure they have for Aaliyah. But we both know that's wishful thinking," Precious commented to Amir.

"I say let's enjoy the peace and quiet, while we can, cause it ain't gonna last. Get prepared to start groveling," Amir advised.

"I already have and it's about to begin now," Precious said, when T-Roc came walking towards them.

"I want to thank you for bringing my grandson home." Were the first words out of T-Roc's mouth, once he was standing in front of Precious and Amir. "I don't think I've ever seen Chantal this happy in my life," he remarked, glancing back at his wife holding baby Desi.

"I understand why. You have a very special grandchild. I only spent a limited time with him and fell in love." Precious stated sincerely.

"So did I," Amir admitted.

"T-Roc, there's no sense in pretending Desi miraculously fell into my arms. We're all aware of the role Aaliyah played in his kidnapping but I'm begging you to show my daughter some mercy. Please..."

T-Roc put his hand up. "Stop."

Precious knew his wrath was coming but she hoped T-Roc would at least give her a chance to plead her case, before cutting her off.

"T-Roc, out of respect, can you allow Precious to express herself. This is difficult for her too," Amir wanted him to know.

"Thank you, Amir but T-Roc has the right to vent. If I was in his position, I'd be furious too."

"Can you both stop speaking for me and let me talk for myself," T-Roc said, shutting them down before sharing his thoughts. "I don't know what Aaliyah was thinking, when she came up with the idea to kidnap Justina's baby. But I've known her since she was a little girl and for her to do something of this magnitude, she must've been in tremendous pain. For that reason, I'm going to give your child the forgiveness, you never showed my wife or my daughter, Precious."

"Ouch, that cut deep but I more than deserved the jab. I never did forgive Chantal or Justina and honestly, I never even tried. I guess we're never too old to learn something because if the notorious and ruthless T-Roc can show forgiveness, then I have no excuse for not attempting to do the same." Precious owned her shortcomings.

"Time will tell if you're being sincere but for now, I'll take your word for it. Now if you excuse me, I'ma go upstairs and wake up Justina and let her know Desi is finally home."

"We had no idea Justina was here. Can I please speak to her before we go?" Precious requested.

"Keep it short, Precious. She hasn't seen her son in weeks."

"I totally understand. I promise I won't take up a lot of her time," Precious assured T-Roc, before he went upstairs.

"I had no idea Justina would be here," Amir mumbled, uneasy about seeing her.

"Why is that a problem for you?"

"Of course not but I haven't seen Justina since we broke up."

"I forgot you still have a thing for her. Well, get over it, Amir. Justina has a child with another man and they're married. She's moved on and so should you."

"I'm well aware of that but it doesn't make it any easier. But I'm a grown man, I can deal," Amir scoffed.

"Chantal, did Justina tell you she was going out?" T-Roc questioned, running down the stairs. Precious could sense a feeling of panic coming from him.

"No! Justina said she was going to bed. She's not in her room?"

"I checked everywhere upstairs and she's not here."

"Unless she took the back elevator, without letting us know," Chantal said nervously.

"She's not answering her phone," T-Roc huffed. "Precious, call Aaliyah."

"You think Justina went after Aaliyah?!" Precious became alarmed.

"All I know is I checked on Justina shortly before you came over and she was in her room resting. Now she's gone," T-Roc said, trying to call her again.

"Aaliyah isn't answering her phone either. Damn! Pick up," she mouthed.

"Fuck! Fuck! Fuck!" T-Roc belted.

"Keep your voice down! You're startling the baby," Chantal warned being protective of her grandchild.

"What if Justina woke up and heard us talking down here. She probably figured Aaliyah came back too," T-Roc rationalized.

"Does Justina know where Aaliyah's townhouse is?" Amir questioned.

"Yes, she does," T-Roc nodded. "Chantal, you stay here with Desi, while I go find Justina."

T-Roc, Precious and Amir rushed out on a mission to locate Justina and Aaliyah. Each of them were praying to find both women unharmed. Given the bad blood between them, they knew it was highly unlikely.

Chapter Eleven

Worst Behavior

When Justina arrived at Aaliyah's townhouse, she parked directly across the street. Her initial reaction was to run up on her spot, use a bat, gun and foot to kick the door down. After careful consideration, she decided that would bring unwanted attention. So, for the next ten minutes, Justina sat in her car and debated what her next move should be.

I should just go back to my parent's house and be with my son. Precious and Amir brought my baby home safely, that's the most important thing,

Justina said to herself. *But I'm sure they're over there right now, begging my dad to forgive Aaliyah and to ask me to do the same, so her trifling ass doesn't go to jail. I'm so sick of her always playing the victim and people giving her a pass, when she's nothing but a self-absorbed, spoiled bitch! If I'd been the one who kidnapped Aaliyah's baby, Precious would be the first person demanding they throw me under the jail, so fuckin' hypocritical!* Justina fumed, getting herself even more worked up.

"Take a deep breath and relax, Justina," she said out loud, trying to calm herself down. She was having flashbacks to all the words of wisdom her father had bestowed upon her these last couple months. "Daddy, I want to make you proud, I really do," Justina muttered, noticing all of his missed calls. She wiped away a tear and decided seeking revenge against Aaliyah wasn't the answer, going home and holding Desi again was. Justina put her foot on the break and was about to hit the start button on her car, when she noticed a familiar face coming around the corner.

"I see you still like taking those nighttime runs, Aaliyah," Justina scoffed, grabbing her gun and throwing her voice of reason out the window.

Aaliyah was listening to music and felt safe in her quiet treelined neighborhood. The run was exactly what she needed to take her mind off all that went wrong in the last forty-eight hours. She reached in a small compartment in the waistband of her running leggings to get her key.

Justina had quietly snuck up behind an unsuspecting Aaliyah. Making sure to wait until she actually unlocked the door before making her move. Like a cat prowling in the night, Justina attacked her prey the moment the door opened. She leaped on top of Aaliyah's back, using the weight of her body to keep her face pressed to the floor.

"Get ready to die!" Justina roared, pressing the barrel of her gun against Aaliyah's head. "You stole my son and really thought you'd get away with it. The joke is on you!"

"Justina, my mother and Amir are bringing your son home as we speak. Elijah might already be at your parent's house right now," Aaliyah said, gasping for air.

"His name is Desi! He was named after his father Desmond Blackwell not fuckin' Elijah, you sick fuck!" Justina screamed, knocking Aaliyah in the back of the head with her gun.

Aaliyah yelled out in pain. She could feel

an open gash in her head and the warm blood dripping down, mixing with the sweat on her face. "You're right...I'm sorry," Aaliyah managed to say through her pain.

"You always talked about how sick and crazy my mother was and that I was just like her but what's your excuse, Aaliyah? What type of woman steals another woman's child? Explain that to me. You even got a fake birth certificate, listing you as his mother! I guess I should've just handed you my husband too, then you can take over my whole fuckin' life. You're pathetic! I'm sure Dale's turning in his grave right now!"

That last comment from her nemesis, sent Aaliyah reeling. She swung her arm wildly, hitting Justina in her ear. Caught up in her own rage, spewing her frustrations made Justina completely unprepared when Aaliyah decided to strike back. She swung on Justina again, this time knocking the gun out her hand.

Justina leaped to the floor, trying to retrieve the weapon but Aaliyah grabbed her leg, pulling her back towards her.

"Get off me!" Justina yelled, stomping her Nike shoe to hit Aaliyah in the face but instead, Aaliyah let her leg go and made her own go for the gun. Both women struggled to stand up, so they crawled but Aaliyah was winning the race which prompted Justina to grab Aaliyah's ponytail to slow her down, only pissing Aaliyah off more.

"You wanna fuck with me! Watch me end you!" Aaliyah balled up her fist, landing a right hook across Justina's cheek. The powerful punch caused her to fall back and Aaliyah took full advantage. She jumped on top of her former best friend and started choking her. Aaliyah was blinded by rage, watching the life drain from Justina's face.

But Justina wasn't ready to surrender to defeat. She tried digging her nails into Aaliyah's eyes, making her loosen the grip around her throat. Justina coughed profusely but also regained enough strength to land her own punch across Aaliyah's nose. When Aaliyah reached up to dab the blood coming from her nose, Justina pushed Aaliyah off and stood up.

"I'm not done with you!" Aaliyah jumped up and swung on Justina and she swung right back. The women continued exchanging blows. They were both bruised, battered and tired ass fuck. But the mutual hatred they shared for one another, kept their adrenaline pumping. Aaliyah and Justina were willing to fight to the death of them.

"Damn, they went all out!" Floyd cracked when he and Caleb entered the venue for Amelia's birthday party.

"I'm wondering who thought it was a good idea to have a kid's party at a nightclub. I put my money on ratchet ass Celinda," Caleb shook his head.

"Man, you made it!" Prevan walked up, hugging his brother.

"You already know I ain't missing my niece's party. Where she at? We got plenty of presents for her," Caleb said holding up some bags.

"She's in the back dressing room with Celinda, changing outfits," Prevan stated.

"Changing outfits?" Floyd gave Prevan a strange look.

"Yeah, Celinda got her one outfit for earlier and another for the nighttime festivities," Prevan smiled.

"You joking or are you serious?" Floyd wanted to know.

"I'm dead ass serious. Celinda just wanted to make sure Amelia had a good time."

"Ain't she like four," Floyd raised an eyebrow.

"I'm sure it was Celinda's idea to have the birthday party at this club too, with all this rap music playing. If there wasn't so much pink princess shit, I would swear this party was for Celinda and not Amelia," Caleb sighed. "What tha fuck am I sayin', Celinda do think she a princess," he remarked, gritting his teeth.

"Can we not do this shit today. It's about Amelia. Play nice," Prevan pleaded with his brother.

"I'll be on my best behavior," Caleb agreed, glancing over at Floyd.

"Appreciate it. Now come back and say what's up to everybody, they been waiting on you," Prevan grinned proudly. It was true. Caleb was a local celebrity. Everyone in Philly knew his name even if they didn't recognize his face but Caleb preferred it that way. He tried to keep a low profile but when you young, rich and good looking, it's hard to stay under the radar.

"Yo, is that Mia running towards you?" Floyd asked Caleb in a low tone. He wasn't sure because even though Mia was always a pretty girl, it was a demure pretty. Now she resembled a Fashion Nova model but without all the plastic and filters.

Caleb nodded his head yes, as Mia ran up

with a wide smile on her face.

"I was starting to think you weren't coming. I'm so glad you made it!" Mia beamed, gazing in Caleb's eyes. "How have you been?"

"I'm cool, just workin' and shit. How 'bout you?"

"I'm good. Just juggling school and work. I got a second job at that new restaurant downtown and the tips have been great, so I'm happy about that."

"Glad to hear you still hittin' those books. If you ever need any financial help, you know I got you." Caleb let Mia know.

"Thank you. That means a lot," Mia smiled sweetly.

"I see my niece. I'll talk to you later," Caleb said, walking off.

"Damn, you ain't gon' neva give that broad a chance," Floyd shook his head as they walked off, leaving Mia standing alone looking devastated. But unlike before, Mia wasn't taking no for an answer. She waited patiently as Caleb lifted his niece up in the air, twirling her around and showered her with birthday gifts. Once Amelia ran off to play with some of her friends, Mia made her move.

"Caleb, can I speak with you for a second?"

Mia asked but this time she didn't have the typical giddy expression on her face.

"Yeah, go 'head and speak," he said casually.

"I meant alone," she replied, glancing over at Floyd who rarely left Caleb's side.

"Ok." Caleb looked over at Floyd, who shrugged his shoulders. Caleb followed behind Mia as she led him to a private booth on the other side of the club. "I guess you really wanted some privacy," he cracked, sitting down across from her.

"Yeah, I don't want us to be interrupted." Mia stated with seriousness.

"Okay, you got me alone. What' on yo' mind, Mia?"

"Why don't you want me, Caleb?"

"Excuse me?" Caleb wasn't expecting Mia to be so direct with her question.

"You heard me. At first I thought it was because I was too plain and didn't look all glamorous and sexy like that girl who came to your birthday party."

Caleb paused for a minute, thinking what tha fuck is this chick talking about because his birthday party was so long ago. He could barely remember what happened last week, let alone months ago. "Oh, you talkin' 'bout Shiffon," he mumbled, remembering how good she looked that night.

"I guess that's her name," Mia snapped, showing her jealously. As she remembered how in lust Caleb seemed that night, when he saw the woman walk in the club. "But yeah, I figured you didn't want a girl who looked plain like me, so I stepped my game up."

Mia glanced down at the multi striped skinny leg jumpsuit, with a halter tie, deep v surplice and belt that cinched her waist. The form fitting jumper accentuated curves that no one knew Mia even had. Her long black hair was in a half up, half down style and she even invested in some Fenty makeup, to enhance her features and take it up a notch.

"Mia, no doubt you a pretty girl but..." Caleb hesitated.

"But what? You've never been one to bite your tongue, so just say it," Mia pushed.

"I can't stand yo' fuckin' sister. I only tolerate her cause of Prevan. If I was dealin' wit' you, I'd have to see her face even more. I can't imagine that shit." Caleb shook his head, becoming agitated at the very thought.

"You can't separate my sister from me?" Mia asked.

"Nah. Can't do it."

"We're not a package deal, Caleb. I'm my own person. Celinda don't define me!" Mia rebuffed.

"I ain't say all that. But it don't change the fact, I don't like her ass and don't wanna see her no more than I have to. Wish that was neva but hey," Caleb shrugged.

"So if there was no Celinda, you saying we could be together?" Mia didn't try to conceal her frustration by what Caleb was saying to her.

"Maybe but don't none of that shit matter. Celinda is here and her trifling ass ain't going nowhere, so ain't no need in speculating."

Caleb noticed Mia's eyes watering up. He wanted to get up and immediately make his exit but a tinge of guilt hit him hard. He'd known Celinda's little sister for years and had love for her but not the type of love she was looking for. It would've been easy for Caleb to just hit a few times and curve her but Mia was like family, so the remorse would be swift.

"You a beautiful, sweet girl. A nigga gon' feel lucky to wife you up but it can't be me. Don't take it personally, Mia. Like I told you earlier, if you need anything, I got you." Caleb leaned over the table and kissed Mia on the cheek before walking away.

"Yeah, I can have anything but you," Mia mumbled as Caleb walked back over to the other side of the club. No matter how many times he shot her down, Mia wasn't ready to give up on her goal of making Caleb her man. She truly believed she was the perfect woman for him. She was on the verge of becoming borderline obsessed with the idea. But like Caleb stated, her pesky sister wasn't going anywhere, so if she couldn't get rid of Celinda then Mia was determined to find another way to get what she wanted.

Chapter Twelve

The Dark Side

"The front door is wide open! Oh fuck, this isn't good!" Precious cried out in fear, when T-Roc pulled up. He didn't even bother parking. He quickly turned off the ignition, put on the emergency lights and they all jumped out, running towards Aaliyah's place.

"I pray we're not too late." Amir said under his breath, thinking the worst but hoping for the best.

"Justina!"

"Aaliyah!"

T-Roc and Precious shouted their daughter's names simultaneously. What they witnessed broke their hearts. Aaliyah and Justina both looked like they had gone twelve rounds with professional boxers. Only their fury for each other, fueled them with enough energy to remain standing.

"Daddy, you need to go!" Justina shouted, keeping her gun aimed at Aaliyah.

"Justina, what are you doing? We talked about this," T-Roc spoke with great sadness in his voice.

"Aaliyah, are you okay?" Precious asked, stepping forward.

"Get back or I'll put a bullet in her!" Justina yelled even louder.

"Mother, I'm fine," Aaliyah uttered, too exhausted to say much more.

"Put down the gun, Justina. You don't want to do this," T-Roc stressed to her.

"But I do. She deserves it. She had Desi's nanny drug me, steal my son and was planning to leave the country with him. I almost lost my mind because of this piece of shit!" Justina spit on the floor where Aaliyah stood. "She doesn't deserve to live!"

"Justina, you might be right but what about

your beautiful son?" Amir came closer, showing his face.

"Stay out of this, Amir! This has nothing to do with you."

"But it does. Just because we're not together anymore, doesn't mean I don't still care about you. You have too much to live for. Don't throw your life away like this." Amir tried his best to give a compelling argument but Justina wasn't trying to hear it.

"Just shut up! All of you! This is between me and Aaliyah! Just go! All of you just go!" Justina screamed, tightening her grip on the trigger.

"We're not going anywhere. If you kill Aaliyah, you will have to do in front of all of us, including me." T-Roc made clear. "Is that what you want your father to see. His only daughter, killing another human being?"

"Daddy stop!"

"You have a beautiful son, waiting to be reunited with his mother but you're willing to throw it all away and spend the rest of your life in prison, for murder. That makes what you're doing, no better than what Aaliyah did."

Those words resonated deeply with Justina. Flashes of seeing little Desi coming to visit her behind bars, made her sick to her stomach. For the first time, since regaining the upper hand in their fight to the death, Justina relaxed her stance but Aaliyah wasn't taking any chances with her life. She leaped forward, trying to yank the gun away from her adversary. The women struggled with the gun and then silence filled the room, when a shot was fired.

The room seemed to be frozen. No one was sure what happened, until T-Roc lifted his hand and there was blood covering his shirt. Justina immediately released the gun from her grasp and ran to her father.

"Daddy! Daddy! I'm so, so sorry. This is all my fault!" Justina cried.

"It's okay," T-Roc said calmly, sitting down on a chair. I just took a bullet in the shoulder," he explained, immediately applying pressure.

"Come on, let's get you fixed up," Amir said, helping T-Roc. "Precious, will you and Aaliyah be okay? I'ma take T-Roc to get his gunshot wound taken care of."

"We're fine," they both nodded. "You go ahead. Let me know how everything goes," Precious said, hugging onto her daughter.

"T-Roc, I'm sorry," Aaliyah called out, as he walked past her, with Justina holding his hand. He simply nodded his head, without saying a word.

"Are you sure you're okay?" Precious asked Aaliyah again, after everyone left.

"I'm fine. I'm not the one who left here with a bullet," Aaliyah huffed, going into the kitchen to get a bottle of water. "Can I get you something?" she casually asked her mother, seeming to emotionally distant herself from what just happened.

"I don't think what you have is strong enough for what I need right now," Precious sighed. "This whole ordeal has been a complete nightmare but what's scarier is, it could've ended up a lot worst."

"Who you telling. I really believed Justina was gonna kill me. She had so much hate in her eyes."

"Can you really blame her, Aaliyah?"

"Are you seriously defending her?!" Aaliyah balked. "She almost killed me!" She spit with indignation.

"I'm not defending Justina but you're not innocent in this either. You had her son kidnapped."

"And I also gave him back."

"Not voluntarily," Precious reminded her headstrong daughter.

"Whatever," Aaliyah cringed. "Justina can now go back to her perfect life, with her beautiful son and rich husband. Since she couldn't kill me, I'm sure she's plotting right now, when would be the perfect time to turn me in to the police on kidnapping charges. Justina will probably make the call right after they drop her daddy off. Instead of a grave, I guess a jail cell will have to suffice," she spewed.

"This rivalry between you and Justina has to end. It's one thing to take her boyfriend, it's another to take her child. There's no reason for you all to be in competition with each other," Precious emphasized to Aaliyah.

"You're absolutely right because there is no competition. Justina is still the same insecure, plain jane girl, wearing glasses, she was when we were growing up. Just because she learned how to put on some makeup, do her hair and wear sexy clothes, doesn't change who she is deep down inside," Aaliyah fussed.

"For argument sake, let's say everything you're yelling about is true. The point is, we all need to start healing, especially you, Aaliyah."

"I can't do that if I'm locked up!"

"T-Roc promised he would make sure you wouldn't spend one day in jail," Precious asserted.

"As if he has any control over that neurotic daughter of his." Aaliyah refused to let up.

"Well, T-Roc was able to talk her down from shooting you. He has more influence over Justina then you might think."

"Maybe but I don't trust anyone in that family, including T-Roc."

"Aaliyah, let's not think about any of that right now." Precious was in no mood to debate her daughter. "I'm emotionally drained and I'm sure you are too. Right now, you should rest."

"I agree. I'm going upstairs to take a long hot bath."

"Sounds like a good idea, sweetheart."

"And mom," Aaliyah stopped herself before going upstairs. "Thank you. You always come through for me. I don't know what I would do without you," she said, giving Precious a hug and kiss.

"You won't ever have to worry about that. I'm your mother. I'll always be here for you...no matter what."

Precious laid back on the couch and closed her eyes after Aaliyah went upstairs. She loved her daughter more than anything. After everything they went through today and surviving it, instead of feeling relieved, she was flooded with anxiety. It concerned her that instead of seeming remorseful for what happened, Aaliyah was angry. Precious was determined to figure out a way to help her daughter start healing, before she swayed over to the dark side and never came back.

"She's getting so big," Talisa smiled, sitting down next to Genesis on the living room sofa as he held Genevieve.

"She really is. It seems like yesterday I was holding this tiny, beautiful baby in my arms after delivering her and all I wanted to do was protect her. Now she's walking and trying to talk. Only time Genevieve's quiet is when she's sleeping." Genesis gave a slight laugh.

"The time does fly, so you have to appreciate every moment." Talisa glided her hand over Genevieve's hair. "She really is a beautiful baby. She looks so much like you and Skylar too."

"When I was playing with her earlier, I was thinking the same thing. How much you know..." Genesis's voice faded.

"It's okay for you to talk about Skylar. I know you cared about her, even loved her. I also know, you're hurting right now. But I want to be here for you, Genesis. Don't shut me out because you're afraid you'll hurt my feelings. I know what we share." Talisa placed her hand over Genesis's hand.

"I can get past the hurt. It's the guilt that's eatin' me up on the inside," Genesis admitted. "I shoulda done more to protect her. Skylar is dead because of me."

"No. This is not your fault. You can't do this to yourself."

"How can I not. I couldn't protect Skylar. What if I can't protect Genevieve either...or you. If anything happened to you again or her," Genesis glanced down at his baby girl, "I wouldn't survive it."

"Genesis, don't..."

"Hold Genevieve. I have to take this call," Genesis said, cutting Talisa off.

"Of course." Talisa noticed her husband answered the call from the phone he used strictly for business. She immediately wondered who was on the other end because Genesis seemed anxious, which was rare.

"It's about time you called me back," Genesis scoffed, going into his office for privacy. "Tell me you found that muthafucka!" He was waiting for Bloodhound to respond but received an dismal surprise.

"Yeah, that nigga found me but unfortunately for him, I found his ass first," Maverick chuckled into the phone. "Rip off that tape," he ordered one of his henchmen. "Bloodhound, say hello to yo' boss."

"Fuck you muthafuckas!" Genesis heard Bloodhound roar at Maverick and his men. Then he heard a loud thump and Bloodhound's voice bellowed through the phone as a baseball bat connected with the back of his head.

"Ain't no denying that nigga gotta lot of heart," Maverick praised. "You should be proud. He takin' this beatin' like a champ. Now cover that nigga's mouth back up."

Genesis gritted his teeth. He wanted to pound his fist in the wall but kept his composure. "This ain't gon' end well for you, Maverick," he warned.

"Maybe it will...maybe it won't but right now I keep gettin' all the wins and you takin' nothing but L's." Maverick taunted.

"You done took this shit too far. It's one thing comin' for my partners but the mother of my child." You could hear the rage in Genesis's voice.

"You shoulda thought about that before you had my crew wiped out. Them niggas had seeds too. You gave zero fucks you was leaving those kids fatherless. So yeah, the mother of yo' daughter is no longer here but would you rather it been yo' wife?" Maverick countered.

The underlining threat sent a chill down Genesis's spine. "I'ma personally put a bullet in yo' fuckin' head."

"I'ma hold you to that. I tell you what. If I die first, just put my money in the grave and I'll do the same for you." Maverick stated arrogantly. "You know...if you meet yo' demise before I do... Deal?" his proposition sounded more like a death sentence.

"It's a deal, muthafucka. I'll make sure you buried wit' all the money you got, when they put you six feet under. Now get ready to die," Genesis promised right before he heard a barrage of shots.

"Let the games begin." Maverick stated after ordering his henchmen to kill Bloodhound. They riddled his upper torso with bullets, leaving his chest ripped open, oozing blood. Bloodhound was another name added to the mounting pile of dead bodies.

Chapter Thirteen

Over It

"Girl, you ain't got no food up in this place," Celinda smacked, closing the refrigerator door.

"Between work, school and this internship at the research lab, I haven't had time to go grocery shopping. Plus, I don't get paid until Friday," Mia said, putting down the book she was reading before her sister popped up unexpectedly.

"When you gon' get you a man? You too cute to be over here struggling all the time. I mean you still ain't even got no furniture in this crib." Celinda frowned up her face, glancing around her sister's cramped one bedroom apartment.

"Working two jobs and going to school full time, leaves little time for dating," Mia shot back.

"I bet if that date was with Caleb yo' ass would make time," Celinda popped.

"Whatever."

"Girl, please. I saw you hiding in the corner booth with Caleb at Amelia's birthday party. You think I ain't never noticed you looking at him like a lost puppy. I get why you like him. He fine and rich."

"It ain't about his money!" Mia slipped and said.

"I knew you liked him!" Celinda pointed her finger at Mia, cheesing hard that she tricked her sister into admitting the truth.

"So what if I like Caleb." Mia cut her eyes at Celinda, wishing she would shut up.

"What's the point of liking a nigga that ain't gon' neva like you back."

"Huh?" Mia couldn't mask the hurt look on her face, by what her sister said.

"Come on, Mia. You know Caleb ain't interested in you. You cute and all but a nigga like Caleb, he wants a woman. Not some lil' college girl."

Celinda's words cut deep. She knew Mia was

a late bloomer and was always insecure about her looks. She liked taking jabs at her baby sister, especially now, since Celinda was the one feeling insecure. Her once awkward sister had suddenly blossomed into a beautiful butterfly. But not only had Mia changed physically, she had a new attitude too. She was no longer willing to let her big sister bully her.

"Caleb not being interested has nothing to do with me. It's because I'm related to you. He thinks you're poison. But you already knew that," Mia quipped.

"Fuck Caleb bitch ass!" Celinda shouted, jumping up from the couch. "I have to go pick up Amelia," she continued, grabbing her purse with a stank attitude.

"Don't let me keep you. You better go pick up your daughter. Since you such a great mother and all," Mia remarked sarcastically.

"Are you tryna say I ain't a good mother?!" Celinda was twisting her neck and flinging her hands like she was ready to brawl.

"You need to calm down and go get my niece. Plus, I need to study for my chemistry test tomorrow, so I ain't got time to argue with you, Celinda." Mia was now standing at the door, holding it wide open.

"I'll go but so you know, if Caleb really wanted you, he wouldn't let his feelings for me stand in the way. He don't wanna hurt yo' feelings but I'ma give it to you straight. That nigga just ain't into you," Celinda smirked. "Oh and one more thing," she continued to twist the knife. "All that studying you doin' to be a chemist, you betta off learning how to cook some drugs. Cause ain't nobody tryna pay you no real money, even after you get a degree," Celinda laughed, before leaving out.

Mia slammed the door and leaned back on the wall. She wanted to cry but her anger wouldn't allow it. A part of her did believe what Celinda said was true. There was always this little voice in her ear whispering she wasn't pretty enough or sexy enough and Caleb wanted someone like Shiffon, the woman she saw him with at his birthday party. As hard as Mia tried not to let her mind play tricks on her, she was allowing her insecurities win the battle. But even while second guessing herself, she wasn't ready to give up on him. Mia decided she just had to figure out how to breakthrough to Caleb. Once she did, he would give their love a chance.

"Thanks for meeting with me on such short notice," Shiffon said when Caleb arrived at the restaurant in downtown Philly.

"Of course I came. You said it was important." Caleb sat down. "Tell me you got some good news regarding Maverick... like that nigga dead."

"No he's not dead but I did want to speak with you about Maverick."

"What about him?"

"I have to get back to Atlanta, so I won't be able to continue on with the job."

"Are you serious? Is it another gig? I told you Genesis will pay whatever."

"It's not about the money, Caleb."

"Isn't it always about the money wit' you, Shiffon. I don't mean that on no negative shit. You about yo' business...like me."

"Normally it is about the money but..." Shiffon stopped herself before continuing.

"But what... is there something else... something you not telling me?" Caleb questioned.

Yeah, I've been having sex with my target. Not only have we been involved intimately but I fell in love with him. I had an opportunity to kill

Maverick but I couldn't pull the trigger, Shiffon thought to herself.

"Yes, there is something else. My mother is having some personal issues and she needs me to come home," she lied and said. Shiffon knew Caleb would find that explanation much more acceptable than the truth.

"Shiffon, I'm so sorry. Is she gonna be okay?"

"Oh no, she's not dying or sick or anything," Shiffon quickly said, seeing the concern on Caleb's face. "She's just going through a difficult time and also needs help with my little brother."

Being a professional killer, Shiffon was used to lying for a living without hesitation but for some reason she felt guilty about lying to Caleb. Maybe it was because she knew he liked her and she did have feelings for him too. But he didn't have her heart, Maverick did.

"I understand. Family should always be yo' top priority. I'm learning that more when I see everything Genesis is going through." Caleb shook his head before becoming distracted by a text message. "Yo, I gotta go!" He sounded frantic.

"Caleb, what's wrong?"

"I just got a 911 text from Floyd. I gotta get to the warehouse," he explained.

"I'll come with you!" Shiffon grabbed her purse and followed behind Caleb as he sprinted out the door.

When Caleb and Shiffon arrived to the warehouse on E Dunton Street, from the outside it appeared deserted.

"It doesn't look like anyone is here," Shiffon said as they were walking toward the entrance.

"Floyd parks around back a lot of times. But in his text, he put 911 warehouse and he ain't answering his phone. I doubt he would leave without hittin' me back," Caleb rationalized.

"True but…" before Shiffon could finish her sentence, from the corner of her eye, she noticed a figure lurking the moment they walked through the door. Within seconds, Shiffon had reached in her purse and retrieved her gun. "Caleb get down!" She yelled, while letting off two shots.

"Fuck!" Caleb muttered taken aback by the ambush. Shiffon's bullets made contact and the man's body dropped to the ground. Another shooter was right behind him but Shiffon was bent down in a corner and put a bullet in his inner thigh. The impact caused the man's legs to buckle, allowing her to put a fatal shot to his dome.

They then heard the sound of footsteps racing out the backdoor. Before Caleb could say a word, Shiffon had bolted off to catch the culprit. He then rushed to catch her. By the time they got outside, they saw a car speeding off. Shiffon was about to bust some more shots but Caleb stopped her.

"Hold up! That's Floyd's car!" Caleb barked. "That might be him driving off."

"Sorry, I was in work mode," Shiffon sighed, putting her gun down. "He probably ran off thinking we were coming to kill him next."

"Yeah, let me call him again. Damn nigga, pick up!" Caleb shouted when the phone rang a few times and then went to voicemail.

"You keep trying to get in touch with Floyd. I'ma go back inside and see if the two men I killed have any identification on them," Shiiffon said, reentering the warehouse. Caleb nodded his head as he continued calling Floyd and also sent him text messages.

As Shiffon headed towards the dead bodies she heard the sound of a cell phone. She immediately aimed her gun thinking there might be another perpetrator lurking. She walked quietly in the direction of the ringing sound. When Shiffon got closer her heart dropped. Floyd laid dead with a shot to the back of the head, execution style. Shiffon was in such a state of shock, she didn't hear anyone come back in. It wasn't until the most gut wrenching roar echoed through the warehouse did she notice Caleb standing behind her.

"Not my nigga Floyd!" Caleb stood frozen in horror, seeing someone he considered a brother lying in a pool of his own blood. Shiffon wanted to comfort him but knew there was nothing she could say that would bring him solace. She watched in agony as Caleb held his best friend since childhood lifeless body in his arms. It was beyond heartbreaking for her to witness someone she cared about be in such excruciating pain. Shiffon knew Caleb's life would never be the same again.

Chapter Fourteen

Confessions

When Precious stepped out the shower she was planning to have a glass of wine, relax in bed and get some much needed rest. Between Skylar's death and spending as much time as possible with Aaliyah in order to keep a watchful eye on her, she was becoming mentally and physically drained. Not only that, she yearned for the day she would see Supreme again. Precious decided to listen to some music, specifically old love songs she adored to help unwind before falling asleep. But when *A Dream* by Debarge came on, her heart fluttered. As she continued to listen to the lyrics her eyes teared up.

A dream, a simple fantasy (It's just a fantasy)
That I wished was reality (That I)
(That you'd come knocking at my door)
That you'd come knocking at my door
(Oh, and then we'd) And we'd relive this dream
once more

A dream

Hold me, love me
With all your heart
Oh, oh-oh, come back
Please make my dream come true for me
I need so much for you to see
I need you to love me once again...

When the bedroom door opened and Precious saw Supreme standing there, for a brief moment she thought her mind was playing tricks on her. Just like the lyrics to the song, this was all a dream.

"I missed you baby." Those four simple words Supreme spoke was all Precious needed to hear to know she wasn't dreaming. Her husband was finally home.

"Do you know how worried I was!" Precious ran over to Supreme and kissed him. Savoring feeling the touch of his lips against hers and his strong arms wrapped around her body. "You better not ever leave me for this long again."

"I won't...I promise," Supreme said, returning his wife's passionate kisses. Precious began to undress her husband, longing to feel him inside her but he tensed up.

"What's wrong...why are you pulling away?" she wanted to know. "I would think you'd be just as ready as I am to get in bed," Precious said glancing back at the inviting silk sheets and burning Jo Malone London Pomegranate Noir Luxury candles.

"Of course I wanna lay you down but..."

"Not a but," Precious cut Supreme off. "I know a lot has happened since we've been apart but let's talk about the bad tomorrow. Tonight, I just want my husband to make love to me."

Supreme was so tempted to oblige his wife's request but his conscious wouldn't let him. "Precious, it's Nico."

"Nico, what about Nico? Oh fuck, did the two of you have another altercation?" Precious huffed. "Babe, at some point these male ego driven disputes have to stop," she shook her head, walking over towards the bed.

"I wish it was that simple." A sadness spread across Supreme's face. It was a look Precious was familiar with but never did she think she would see it when her husband was discussing Nico.

"What are you tryna tell me?"

"Nico was shot and he's been in a coma. He's had numerous surgeries but he hasn't gotten any better. The doctor says there's nothing more he can do," Supreme stated somberly.

"Then find another doctor who can perform another surgery," Precious shot back defiantly.

"I've spoken to some of the best surgeons in the world. I even flew a couple in. I know you don't want to hear this and it's breaking my heart to tell you but the only thing that's keeping Nico alive right now is a machine."

"No...no." Precious kept shaking her head in denial. "Nico can't be dead. What will I tell Aaliyah? She's already been through so much."

"We'll tell her together. But because her and Angel are the next of kin, they need to be the ones to give consent to pull the plug," Supreme explained.

"This isn't happening. First Quentin, then her unborn child, her husband and now Nico. This is too much. She's already on edge and this will push Aaliyah right over the cliff."

"I understand you're worried and you have every right to be but Aaliyah is a lot stronger than you think. She can survive this."

"You have no idea what has happened since you've been gone. If you only knew half of it, you wouldn't be saying this. Mentally, Aaliyah is extremely fragile."

"Does this have anything to do with what Amir was helping you with?" Supreme asked.

"Amir told you?"

"He wouldn't give up any details. He said it wasn't his place to tell me. That you should be the one."

"He's right. I was hoping we could have one night with no drama but why stop with the depressing news now. Aaliyah kidnapped Justina's son."

"What! This isn't the time to be joking, Precious. Cause that shit ain't funny."

"No it's not. Unfortunately I'm dead ass serious. It was an absolute nightmare. None of us are saints but never did I believe our daughter would steal another woman's child," Precious sighed. "We're lucky T-Roc agreed to make sure Justina didn't press charges."

"Of course he agreed. T-Roc is a lot of things

but he ain't a snitch. Even when it comes to his daughter and grandchild. If anything he would retaliate. But we have a long history, so he'll let it go."

"I agree but the damage is done."

"I can always fix damage. I'm more concerned about Aaliyah." Supreme exhaled.

"Are you wondering if Aaliyah is so damaged that she can't be fixed. Because that's the question I've been asking myself every day and I still don't know the answer," Precious admitted.

Supreme stared up at the ceiling in deep thought. He already had regret about Nico and now he was flooded with guilt because he hadn't been there for Aaliyah. He knew she was hurting but he wondered how he missed the signs that she was so far gone. With Nico no longer being here, Supreme promised himself he would do everything in his power to save their daughter.

"Amir, it's so wonderful to see you." Talisa hugged her son tightly.

"I've been hoping you would come over and visit."

"I knew dad would be away all day, so I

thought it was a good time to stop by and see you," Amir said, sitting down with his mother at the dining room table.

"Have you already had lunch? I can have Bernice make you a plate," Talisa offered.

"No, I'm good Mother. I just wanted to spend some time with you."

"I've been wanting to spend time with you too. I know things are tense between you and your father but give him time, Amir. He'll come around."

"I want to believe you're right but honestly I don't have the luxury of time." Amir's jaw tightened up. "I need dad to be here for me now."

"Is there something wrong, Amir...are you in some type of trouble?"

"Yeah I am."

"Oh, Amir." Talisa reached across the table and held her son's hand. "Is there anything I can do to help? You know I would do anything for you."

Before Amir could respond to his mother, Genesis walked in, startling both of them. "Dad, I thought you were in meetings all day." Amir could tell by the look on his father's face, he wasn't pleased to see him.

"Lorenzo was in town and said he could

handle the rest of the meetings. I wanted to come home and spend time with Genevieve," Genesis said, walking over to his wife and giving her a kiss.

"Well, I'm glad you're home," Talisa beamed. "But I just put Genevieve down for a nap."

"That's fine. I'll just go in and check on her."

"Make sure you don't wake her up," Talisa smiled. "Oh and Amir needed to speak to you about an important matter," Talisa said glancing over at her son.

"Okay. Give me a few minutes to go see Genevieve and he can meet me in my office," Genesis stated, only making eye contact with his wife.

"Mom, why did you say that?" Amir questioned when his father left the room. "I wasn't ready to talk to him just yet."

"Delaying the conversation won't change anything. You said you were in trouble."

"I know but I don't think this is the right time. Dad barely looked at me when he came in." Amir shook his head in frustration.

"You may not be on good terms with your father right now but you're his son and he loves you. If you need his help then he would want to be there for you. Now go and speak with him," Talisa insisted.

"I hope you're right." Amir got up from his chair and walked towards his Father's office. The hallway seemed even longer than usual and Amir kept replaying what he would say until he reached the doorway entrance.

"Come in," Genesis said, noticing Amir standing there. "What do you need to speak to me about?" Genesis was sitting behind his desk and still not making eye contact with his son which made his presence all the more intimidating. Amir knew he needed to get right to his dilemma before his Father changed his mind and asked him to leave.

"You've been dealing with a lot lately, so I haven't had time to discuss a few things with you," he said, taking a seat. "But recently I spent some time with Justina's baby. When I held him, I thought about this one particular picture when I was his age and you were holding me. We looked so much alike. In my heart I knew he was mine," Amir revealed.

"It takes a lot more than a picture to claim a baby as your own," Genesis remarked, not looking up.

"I know. So I had a DNA test done."

"I hope you didn't use the same person who switched the results for Genevieve." His father's comment felt like a gut wrenching punch.

"I deserved that but no I didn't use the same person. These results are solid. Justina's baby is mine. I'm a father."

"Congratulations," Genesis said, half-heartedly.

"It's complicated. I went to see an attorney and because Justina and Desmond were married and his name is on the birth certificate, I have no legal rights. So, I need your help, dad."

"What do you want me to do?"

"Help me get my son. I deserve to have a relationship with him and be in his life. Please help me make that happen," Amir pleaded.

"You tried to strip me of my rights of having a relationship with my own daughter and you come in here and whine about what you deserve. Then you expect me to help you." Genesis was now staring his son directly in his eyes and was clearly appalled by the request.

"Dad, I completely understand what you're saying and you're absolutely right. I'll always regret what I did but please don't let that keep you from helping me. Between T-Roc and Desmond, I'll never be able to win without you. They're too powerful. And don't you want a relationship with your grandson?"

"Don't worry about me. I'm sure I can work something out with Justina and she won't stop me from having a relationship with my grandchild," Genesis announced confidently.

"What about me?"

"What about you," Genesis shrugged.

"You would deny me my right to have a relationship with my own child?"

"You mean the same right you denied me," Genesis nodded. "Unlike what you did, I'm not denying you anything. All I'm saying is you won't have my help to get it done. You want your son, you fight for him on your own."

"But I can't win on my own." Amir got choked up.

"There's a reason why people say don't bite the hand that feeds you. You're learning that lesson the hard way. Now if there's nothing else, you can go now."

The coldness in his father's voice sent a chill down Amir's spine. He got up to leave but before he did, he reached in his wallet and pulled out the photo of his dad holding him when he was a baby. He placed it on his father's desk and left. Genesis wouldn't admit it out loud but he knew exactly what photo Amir had been talking about and it brought back so many memories. Some good and some sad. Especially remembering all those years of raising his son without his mother because he believed Talisa was dead. Now the son he once adored was himself a father but instead of Genesis embracing Amir, he was choosing to let him go.

Chapter Fifteen

I Need Answers

"I wasn't sure you was gon' pick up," Caleb said when Shiffon answered his call. He had just left Floyd's mother's house and was sitting outside in his car, feeling all sorts of fucked up in the head. He hoped speaking to Shiffon would ease the pain, if only even slightly.

"Why would you think that?"

"We haven't spoken since you went back to Atlanta and I don't like the way we parted ways."

"Amir, what are you talking about. Your best friend was murdered. You were grieving. I'm sure you still are."

"I know but I never thanked you for saving my life. If you hadn't been there wit' me and shot them niggas, I would be buried in a grave right next to Floyd. So thank you."

"You welcome but that's what I do. Have you found out who's behind his murder yet?"

"Nah not yet but trust I'm workin' on it."

"Do you think Floyd walked in when the warehouse was being robbed and they killed him or was he the target?" Shiffon asked.

"I'm tryna figure out the same shit. They took the product and they killed my man. The two you shot ain't even local niggaas, so it's not like Floyd could ID them. They coulda let him live. Unless having him killed was always a part of the plan," Caleb presumed.

"True...very true," Shiffon agreed.

"Somebody keep callin' me. Let me take this and call you back."

"Okay but Caleb just know, if you need me, I'll be there." Shiffon wanted to make sure he had no doubts that she cared about him.

"I appreciate that, Shiffon. I'ma hit you back," Caleb said when he saw the number he didn't recognize calling back again. "Yo, who this?"

"My man, Caleb. I was thinkin' I might have

to come see you in person, since you wasn't answering my calls."

"Do I fuckin' know you? If so, say yo' name. If not , why the fuck is you callin' me and what the fuck do you want?"

"Relax nigga. I wanna help you out."

"I'm good. Let me click tha fuck off," Caleb mumbled about to end the call but the man knew exactly what to say to stop that from happening.

"Hold up! Don't you wanna know who killed Floyd."

"What tha fuck you say?!" Caleb was no longer leaning back in the driver's seat of his car. He was sitting up straight on full alert.

"You heard me. If you wanna know who responsible for puttin' a bullet in the back of yo' man's head, you betta listen to what I got to say."

"When you said you were stopping by, you didn't tell me dad was coming with you!" Aaliyah beamed, hugging Supreme. "I missed you so much."

"I missed you too," Supreme smiled, squeezing her tightly. "How you feeling?" he asked as they entered Aaliyah's townhouse with their inner arms locked.

"I'm good. I'm really good."

Precious side eyed her daughter. "I already told Supreme everything, Aaliyah. So you don't have to pretend."

"Dad, I can explain," Aaliyah quickly said once she realized he knew the truth.

"You don't have to explain right now," Supreme said when they sat down in the living room. "I'm more concerned about how you're dealing with the aftermath...emotionally that is."

"Honestly, it's been hard. I feel stuck. I don't know what direction I should take with my life but I know this isn't it. I'm tired of being sad and miserable. I wanna be happy again," Aaliyah admitted.

"You will be." Supreme stroked the side of Aaliyah's arm lovingly, as he contemplated how he would break the devasting news to her.

"How did I forget," Precious uttered, trying to break the somber mood that was only about to get worse. "Maria baked your favorite cookies," she stated enthusiastically. Handing the bag of goodies to her daughter like she was still six years old.

Aaliyah took the bag but Precious and Supreme both noticed her reluctance. "The last time you surprised me with these cookies, is when you paid off a guard to let you sneak them in, when you came to visit me in jail."

"True," Precious nodded, remembering that visit vividly.

"I was miserable and depressed. You said besides getting out of jail, these cookies were the next best thing to make me feel better. At least temporarily. So what gives…Oh no!" Aaliyah dropped the bag of cookies and stood up. "Has Justina decided to press charges against me…Has a warrant been issued for my arrest? I can't go back to jail…I won't!" She screamed.

"Aaliyah, calm down. Nobody is going back to jail," Supreme reassured her. "That situation has been handled."

"Then what is going on? First you all show up together like a pair of suburbia parents and now mom is trying to pacify me with cookies." Aaliyah stood with her arms folded waiting for an answer

"It's your father," Supreme finally said.

"Huh? You are my father." Aaliyah was confused for a brief second, then it hit her. "You mean Nico?" her face became panic stricken. "Please don't tell me something happened to my dad."

Tears instantly filled Aaliyah's eyes. She

knew what would be said next was horrible news. That was the logical explanation for her parents unexpected visit and behavior. Without saying another word, Aaliyah sat back down and bawled her heart out. She could barely hear the words coming out of Supreme's mouth except for, shot, coma and taking her father off life support.

Chapter Sixteen

Truth Hurts

"Yes Papi! This dick feel so good," Celinda purred, riding Prevan like a stallion. She was rubbing on her tits and licking her lips while talking dirty to him in Spanish. At the rate they were going, they were about to make another baby until Caleb put an end to all that.

"Bitch, you wanna die on my brotha's dick or over in that corner?" Caleb barked, with a 9mm pointed to the back of Celinda's head.

Prevan's dick immediately went limp and all you heard was Celinda's ear piercing screaming.

"Shut the fuck up you grimy bitch!" Caleb jammed the tip of the gun in her skull.

"Yo Caleb, what tha fuck is you doing? You done lost yo' fuckin' mind!" Prevan yelled at his brother.

"Nah nigga, this hoe done lost her mind," Caleb spit, pressing the gun with such force against the back of her head, Celinda tumbled forward on Prevan's chest. "You really thought you could set up my best friend...my brother and get away wit' that shit!"

"Okay, everybody calm down." Prevan moved Celinda to the side of the bed. He grabbed his underwear and pants, hoping to be the voice of reason but Caleb wasn't having it.

"Nigga, if you don't shut tha fuck up! Did you not hear what I said? This trifling hoe got Floyd murdered. She the reason he dead. Ain't no calming down gon' happen until this bitch dead. Unless you ready to take this bullet for her, then you best shut tha fuck up," Caleb warned.

Prevan had to take a step back. He knew his little brother had a temper when pushed too far but he'd never seen him this enraged before. Caleb was like a volcano that erupted and there was no containing it. He decided to take a different approach.

"Celinda, just tell Caleb you ain't have nothing to do wit' Floyd's death...go 'head and tell him," Prevan encouraged her but she didn't give the response he was expecting.

"I didn't know they was gonna kill him. He said they was just gonna rob the place!" Celinda wailed. Fear made her admit the truth.

"You knew somebody was gonna rob the warehouse and you didn't say anything?" Prevan sounded stunned. "Why tha fuck would you do that?"

"Nigga, get yo' head out her pussy. This bitch set the shit up. She fuckin' one of Maverick's niggas and gave him all the info he needed," Caleb scoffed, seconds away from pulling the trigger. "This sneaky hoe was supposed to get a cut of whatever they got."

"Is this true Celinda?" Prevan was over there sounding like a wounded dog.

"I just wanted to get a new car for our daughter. Nobody was supposed to die! I'm so, so sorry!" Celinda continued to sob and Caleb was ready to shut her up permanently.

"Man, I had promised her a car," Prevan said, scrambling to find an excuse for Celinda's unforgivable behavior. "I know that don't make what she did right but I know Celinda would neva had been a part of that shit if she knew they would hurt Floyd."

"Did you not hear what I said?" Caleb looked at his brother dumbfounded. "Floyd is dead 'cause she fuckin' another nigga and gave him info on my shit. I would be dead too if it wasn't for Shiffon. Is you not understanding this shit, you pussy whipped muthafucka!"

"I get it," Prevan stuttered. "But what about Amelia. If you kill Celinda, you gon' leave my daughter without a mother."

"Man, I'd be doing my niece a favor. Savages shouldn't raise kids. You can leave now or watch yo' baby mama die. It's up to you," Caleb stated, tightly gripping the barrel of the gun.

"Nooooooo! Prevan, you can't let yo' brother kill me! Amelia needs her mother!" Celinda's tear filled pleas had her crying so loud, Caleb didn't hear his mother come in.

"Prevan, you home!" She called out coming down the hallway towards the bedroom.

"Ms. Jacobs we in here!" Celinda yelled out, hoping Caleb's and Prevan's mother would be her savior.

"What in the world is going on in here?" she was petrified seeing her youngest son pointing a gun at a butt naked Celinda.

"Ma, you need to turn around and go. Now!" Caleb directed.

"Caleb, I don't know what is going on but whatever it is, this ain't how you handle it," she said before being interrupted by her granddaughter running in the house. "Baby, go outside and stay with your Aunt Mia," Ms. Jacobs turned around and said, not wanting Amelia to see what was going on.

"But I want to show mommy and daddy what you bought me from the store!" Amelia said excitedly.

Caleb glared at Celinda. "Don't you say shit." He mouthed to her in a low tone, knowing she would call his niece in the bedroom in order to guarantee her survival. Celinda knew Caleb would never kill her in front of Amelia.

"Mommy and daddy are busy right now but they'll be out shortly and you can show them everything you got from the mall," Ms. Jacobs said taking her granddaughter's hand and leading her out to the living room. "Mia, take Amelia outside."

"But we..." Mia couldn't finish her sentence because she was cut off.

"Just do it!" Ms. Jacobs snapped at Mia as she took her hand and did as she was told. She went rushing back into the bedroom praying she could stop Caleb from committing murder.

"Ma, please talk some sense into Caleb," Prevan insisted.

"Shut tha fuck up, Prevan and Ma stay out this shit. She the reason Floyd is dead and now she gotta go."

"Baby, I understand. You know how I feel about Celinda but think of your niece...my granddaughter. Imagine how devastated she'll be to lose her mother and her uncle too. Because if you pull that trigger you will spend the rest of your life behind bars. I don't want that for you and neither would Floyd. Now put the gun down, son."

Caleb heard every word his mother said and in his heart, he knew she was right. But even with her being the voice of reason, Caleb was determined to end Celinda for good. She was worse than poison, more like an incurable deadly disease. She was the type of chick who would never change. Caleb knew no matter how sorry Celinda said she was, she was damaged goods. For that reason, Caleb decided Celinda had to die.

"Baby, I have to go meet with T-Roc. I should only be gone a couple hours. Maybe when I get back, we can go to that restaurant you love so much for dinner." Genesis told Talisa, as he was getting ready to head out.

"That would be nice," Talisa smiled, putting down the book she was reading. "Are you in a rush? You've been locked away in your office all afternoon and I was hoping we could talk before you go."

"I'm sorry, baby. It's just been one of those days. I have a little time. What did you want to talk about?" Genesis asked sitting down next to his wife.

"Amir."

"I don't wanna do this right now," Genesis said, standing back up.

"Please." Talisa reached out and grabbed her husband's arm. Genesis grudgingly sat back down. "You can't turn your back on our son."

"Me not helping Amir, isn't turning my back on him. He's a grown man. He'll have to figure it out on his own."

"We're talking about our grandson, Genesis."

"Are we? Do we even know the test results are accurate, or did he have them tampered with. We both know he's capable of doing that?"

"Genesis, I saw the picture. He looks exactly like Amir did when he was a baby. Besides, you don't honestly believe he tampered with the DNA results. He is the father of Justina's son and he should raise him."

"Are you suggesting Amir take that baby away from Justina?"

"No, of course not. But they should share custody. Amir has as much right to raise his son as she does."

"That's for a court to decide."

"If your relationship with Amir wasn't strained, you would be willing to move mountains to get his son. You wouldn't give a damn what a court had to say. I refuse to believe you don't care."

"I care just about as much as Amir did, when he went out of his way to keep me from my daughter."

"Yes, he was wrong but at some point you have to forgive our son. You were on that path to forgiveness until Skylar died."

"You mean murdered. Skylar was murdered."

"I guess you want to blame that on our son too. Are you going to just exile him from your life?" Talisa snapped.

"I don't know what you want from me?"

"I want you to be his father. You do realize you have more than one child."

"It was Amir who tried to erase my other child, so it would be all about him."

"You make it sound like this is some competition."

"No, Amir made it a competition. Why else would he do something so vile. All because of his jealousy for my daughter that I shared with another woman, who is now dead," Genesis seethed.

"What he did wasn't because of his jealousy, it was because of me. But I guess you don't want to admit that. If you did, then you would have to sever your relationship with me too. Deep down inside, do you blame me too, Genesis?" Talisa asked her husband.

"I'm not sure what I think anymore but I can tell you what I know as fact. Amir had the DNA test results changed. Skylar is dead and Genevieve needs her father more than ever. Now I have to go."

Talisa was infuriated. She wanted to run

after Genesis and make him stay, so they could finish their conversation and resolve their issues. No matter how angry he was, she wasn't going to allow her husband to let their son go. Yes, Amir was now a grown man but he still needed his father. Not only that, Amir needed his son.

Chapter Seventeen

After The Storm

Once Caleb took the first round from the magazine and put it in chamber, then pulled the trigger, he couldn't stop. He released each bullet as everyone in the room stood silently in disbelief.

"Is everybody okay in here!" Mia came running in the bedroom out of breath.

"Where's Amelia?" Ms. Jacobs yelled, worried about her granddaughter.

"She's fine!" Mia said, glancing around the room nervously. "When I heard the gunshots, I took her across the street to Ms. Walker's house.

What happened?"

"I was about to kill yo' sister but murdered that pillow instead," Caleb said, breathing heavy.

Celinda was huddled in the corner in the fetal position. Thankful to still be alive but scared out of her mind. She had never felt that close to death.

"What did she do now?" Mia questioned, not even bothering to ask if her sister was okay.

"It wasn't my fault!" Celinda whined. "I had no idea they was gon' kill Floyd."

"You the reason Floyd is dead?" Mia stared at her sister in disgust. "Caleb wait!" She called out when he brushed past her, leaving the room. Mia ran after him. "Don't go!"

"I can't be around her for one more second. If I stay, I'ma choke the life outta that bitch. And I can't do that to my mom. She'll blame herself if I spend the rest of my life in jail for murdering that hoe."

"Then let me come with you. You shouldn't be alone right now, Caleb. You need me."

"What I need is for Celinda to be outta my life forever," Caleb said, getting in his car and driving away.

Mia stormed back in the house and made a beeline to her sister. Celinda now had the bedsheet wrapped around her naked body, crying on Prevan's shoulder. Ms. Jacobs was sitting on the edge of the bed still in shock by what had transpired. She just knew her son was about to commit murder, right in front of her eyes and felt helpless to stop him.

"What the fuck is wrong with you Celinda!" Mia shouted, which was out of character for the normally mild mannered girl. "How could you do that? Floyd was a good dude and you know how close he was to Caleb."

"It wasn't my fault!" Celinda continued with the denials.

"If it wasn't your fault, why did Caleb have to get out this house before he fucked around and killed you?" Mia snapped.

Instead of answering her sister's question, Celinda deflected by turning on the waterworks. The tears were flowing steadily, as Prevan tried to console her.

"Mia, I think you should go. Celinda been through enough today. The two of you can hash this shit out some other time," Prevan said holding his baby mama close in his arms.

"I have so much to say but never mind." Mia shook her head and stormed out.

"Boss, what's our next move?" Micah asked Maverick who seemed preoccupied.

"Hold on a minute." He sounded annoyed while responding to a text message from Shiffon. Micah and Cam eyed each other wondering what was more important than business.

"Yo, look who blowin' me up," Cam chuckled, showing Micah one of his burner phones.

"Who?" Maverick questioned, now ready to give his right hand men his full attention.

"That gutter broad, Celinda," Cam answered.

"I'm surprised the bitch ain't dead," Micah remarked. "You sure yo' guy told Caleb everything?"

"Fuckin' right. I was sittin' right there. He laid the shit out for the nigga. Hold up, now she texting me. Oh yeah, that nigga went to see her ass," Cam nodded reading Celinda's text. "She sayin' her baby daddy brother almost killed her," he laughed.

"I wonder why he didn't?" Micah questioned. "I know I woulda killed the bitch."

"It don't matter. She was just used to create disruption and it worked," Maverick stated, staring out the window in the high rise apartment he'd been staying at, keeping a low profile. "Caleb's business has already slowed down since they took out Floyd. His mind ain't right. Trust me, I know the feeling."

"You still haven't told us what our next move is," Micah wanted to know.

"We takin' a trip to Atl. There's someone I need to see before we disappear for a while."

"Disappear...but we haven't got rid of Genesis yet. Ain't all this shit about him and what tha fuck he did." Micah barked.

"Of course and I can promise you, Genesis will be handled. But he on full alert right now. We already started the storm. It's time to fall back for a minute. Let the nigga relax. Then we strike again. But this time we don't bring a storm, it'll be a full blown category 5 hurricane." Maverick gave a devilish grin.

"I like the sound of that," Cam smiled.

"You always know how to make the best moves. Guess that's why you the boss," Micah agreed.

When the driver pulled up in front of T-Roc's

residence, he was about to get out and open the back door for Genesis but noticed his boss was leaning back in deep thought.

"Sir, we're here," he announced and waited for further instructions.

"Give me a few minutes. I need to make a phone call," Genesis told his driver. Making a decision of what to do next.

"Dad, you're the last person I expected to hear from," Amir said, wondering what prompted his father's call.

"I still have some unresolved anger that I need to work through," Genesis said, cutting straight to the point. "But your my first born and I'll always love you, so go get your son and bring him home. You have my full support."

"Dad, I don't know what to say. Thank you. I'll make you proud…I promise. And I won't ever disappoint you again."

"Just do right by my grandson and be the best father you can possibly be. That's all I want you to do and you'll make me proud."

"I will. I put that on everything, dad," Amir promised once more before they ended their call.

"I'm ready. Let's go see T-Roc," Genesis announced, feeling he was finally ready to let go of his anger and work towards forgiving his son.

"Yes sir." The driver stepped out the car and opened the back door for his boss.

Genesis came to see his longtime friend for one reason but now it was for another. He didn't have any intentions of letting T-Roc know what Amir planned on doing because naturally, he'd want to give his daughter a heads up. But Genesis did hope his visit would set a peaceful tone and that no matter where the custody battle between Amir and Justina went, the two men would remain friends.

Chapter Eighteen

Goodbye

Justina was relishing being back home in Miami with her husband and son but also reeling over the stunt her former best friend pulled. Her anger for Aaliyah ran deep and if it wasn't for her father forbidding her to seek retribution, Justina would keep her foot on her enemies throat.

"So, that's the entire story, from beginning to end." Justina stated, sitting on the armchair smiling at her husband and their son.

"And quite a story it is," Desmond said, shaking his head. "I still wish you would've come to me. I should've been there to help you. Dealing with all that craziness by yourself, it angers me."

"Baby, it all worked out and my father was amazing. Honestly, this whole ordeal brought us closer together. I hate this had to happen," Justina said, stroking Desi's hair. "But I truly understand the importance of family now. I love you so much, Desmond. Now more than ever."

"I love you too." He leaned up to kiss his wife.

"You and Desi are my world and nothing will ever tear us apart," Justina swore. "Baby, you stay here with little Desi and I'll get the door," she said getting up.

"Good afternoon, Justina."

"Amir, what are you doing here? I hope you didn't come all this way to check up on me because I'm fine."

"I'm glad to hear that. Can I come in?"

"Of course." Justina stepped to the side, allowing Amir inside the house. "You still haven't told me why you're here," she said, closing the door.

Amir stared over at Desmond who was holding Desi in his arms. He glanced back at Justina before resting his eyes on her husband. "I came here to get my son and I'm not leaving until I do," Amir vowed.

"What do you want?" Celinda huffed when she opened the door and saw her sister standing there. "If you came over here to talk some more shit because of what happened to Floyd, you can just go! I already got a fuckin' headache."

"I actually came over to make a peace offering," Mia smiled holding up two bags. "I brought over some food from your favorite Dominican restaurant and even a bottle of wine."

"Where you get some money from to buy food and liquor," Celinda cracked. "You finally gotta man," she joked, grabbing the bags from her sister.

"I made some great tips last night at work and I wanted to do something nice for my big sister."

"Well, I guess you can come in then."

"Thanks. I really am sorry, Celinda. I know we've had our differences recently but you would never purposely let something happen to Floyd. He was like family," Mia said sitting down with her sister who had already started eating her food.

"I wouldn't say all that but nah, I really didn't know they was gon' kill Floyd. I just wanted the money, so I could buy me a new car. I'm tired of waitin' for Prevan to step up."

"Where is Prevan," Mia said glancing around."

"You already know Amelia spends the weekend with his mother, so he dropped her off and then he was going to see Caleb. That nigga been actin' funny ever since he threatened to blow my head off. I'm the one that should be pissed off at his ass. I was traumatized and he fucked up my pillows."

"I'ma go get us some glasses for the wine," Mia said heading to the kitchen.

"Caleb ain't been givin' Prevan no work. We over here struggling," Celinda continued to fuss. "Hopefully after they talk, Caleb will start giving Prevan product again."

"I'm sure it will work out. I mean they are brothers," Mia said, pouring the wine.

"Oh please that don't mean shit. Family fuck each other over all the time," Celinda rolled her eyes. "Girl, go get me some water. This food good but it taste a little different," she commented sipping her wine. "They do be puttin' mad seasoning in they food. It's making me thirsty."

"It's okay to come up for air," Mia laughed, handing Celinda the water. "You devouring that food in record speed."

"I was starving. I think I'm eatin' too fast. Oh fuuuuuuuck!" Celinda cried out.

"What's wrong?" Mia asked sounding concerned.

"I don't know but all of a sudden I'm in so much fuckin' pain," Celinda moaned, falling off the couch. "I think I need to go to the emergency room," she cried staring up at her sister, begging for help. But instead of helping, Mia sat down and watched her sister die.

Mia used the lethal powdery substance strychnine to end Celinda's life. Strychnine is a white, odorless but somewhat bitter crystalline powder. She added it to her sister's Dominican food. It was imperative she mixed it with food that had a very strong taste to overcome the exceptional bitterness. This poisonous concoction increases the flex of the spinal cord, thereby causing severe contractions of the back muscles. The backward arching becomes so severe that the spinal cord will often break.

"Help me!" Celinda yelled. But she soon realized her sister had no intention of being her savior. She reached to grab her cell phone to call 911.

"You won't be needing that," Mia scoffed, snatching the phone off the table.

"Why...why?" Celinda wept, not wanting to

die, especially not in such an excruciating painful way.

Mia kneeled down so she was eye level with her dying sister. "Because you are an evil bitch who only cares about herself."

"What about Amelia. She needs her mother," Celinda groveled.

"I'm looking out for my niece's best interest. She's better off without you. But I promise to take excellent care of her."

"Fuck you!" Were Celinda's final words before taking her final breath.

"Girl, I can't wait for us to start this new job next week," Essence said to Shiffon as they were leaving Lenox Mall.

"Yeah, I'm ready to get back to work too. We missed out on a couple good paying gigs because of me being in Philly for way longer than I expected," Shiffon said thinking back to the real reason she had been MIA. She had fallen hard for Maverick. But it was time to put that behind her and focus on getting that money.

"Who you tellin'. My pockets are hurting. A bitch needs some coins, so thank fuckin' goodness you back and we getting to work!" Essence cheered. "Girl, are you even listening to me?" she questioned, noticing Shiffon glancing around.

"I feel somebody is watching me."

"You mean like a nigga checkin' you out?" Essence asked.

"No! Like watching me for the last couple days. Tracking my moves," Shiffon clarified.

"Girl, you just paranoid, which is normal due to the line of business we in. I mean we do kill people for a living. It's natural for you to watch yo' back. Ain't that the reason you always carrying a weapon," Essence smacked.

"You have a point," Shiffon said, looking around one more time before getting into the car. "Being a hired assassin can make a bitch paranoid. Let's go have a drink and calm these nerves down," she laughed, driving off.

Maverick watched from a distance as Shiffon drove away. He wanted to see her one last time before he disappeared. Once he went off the grid, he wouldn't contact anyone including the woman he'd caught feelings for. But as much as he wanted to talk to her, hold her and make love one more time, Maverick decided this would be the closest they would get. This was him telling Shiffon goodbye.

Chapter Nineteen

Crazy In Love

"Are you sure you don't want me to come with you tomorrow?" Talisa asked Genesis as he was getting dressed for a meeting.

"No. To be honest I would prefer not to go. I don't wanna be there when they pull the plug on a man I consider to be a brother. But Precious asked me to be there and it's the least I can do."

"I know how hard this is on you. I still can't believe after today Nico will be gone."

"Nico will never be gone. His name will forever ring in these streets, I'll make sure of that."

"I know you will and Nico would've done the same for you because you truly are a good man," Talisa said with love in her eyes. "You've been so busy lately, we really haven't had a chance to talk. Which means, I haven't been able to say thank you for giving Amir your support."

"You don't have to thank me."

"Yes I do. I know you're still hurting by what our son did but you put that aside and I love you even more for doing so," Talisa said kissing her husband.

"I love you even more for showing me how to be a better man...a better father and now a grandfather."

"There's been so much sadness surrounding us lately but Genevieve and now finding out Amir is a father, brings the joy we desperately need."

"I agree. Amir's in Miami now and if everything goes as planned, we'll be meeting our grandson for the first time very soon," Genesis stated proudly.

Genesis had become trapped in a dark place. He hadn't grasped how deeply until he finally saw a glimmer of sunshine upon finding out he was a grandfather. He prayed Amir would bring his son home because it was the new beginning their family needed to survive so much death.

Shiffon was on her way to collect the first half of the retainer fee for Bad Bitches Only new job when she noticed an unknown Philly number calling one of her phones.

"Hello," Shiffon answered with caution.

"Hey, it's me Caleb."

"Caleb, it's good to hear from you. I called you the other day but the number was disconnected. I wanted to make sure you were okay."

"Yeah, this my new number. I meant to call you earlier but I got sidetracked wit' some other shit," Caleb said, thinking back to how close he came to putting a bullet in Celinda's head. He was in no mood to speak to anyone and changed his number.

"I understand. You have a lot going on right now. Have you gotten any leads regarding Floyd?"

"Yeah, I did. That nigga Maverick was behind it."

"Are you sure?" Shiffon had to pull over, so she wouldn't crash her car.

"Fuckin' positive. He had one of his niggas push up on my brother's baby mother and she set Floyd up."

"What kinda foul ass chick is that. I see why you been sidetracked," Shiffon sighed, shaking her head.

"I almost killed that bitch. If my Mother hadn't showed up, she'd be dead right now," Caleb admitted.

"She deserves to die but I'm glad it wasn't by you. My feelings would be hurt if you were locked up, especially behind a grimy broad like that."

"Feelings...I wasn't sure you had those. I'm kiddin'," Caleb quickly added. "But nah, it makes me feel good that you care."

"Of course I care. You should know that."

"Now I do but we can further discuss that next time we see each other in person. I called you about something else."

"Sure, what is it?"

"You know Genesis had one of his investigators tracking Maverick. Well he finally hit pay dirt."

"Really...you know where he is?"

"Yep. That nigga in yo' neck of the woods. He's supposed to be chartering a private jet from Fulton County Airport-Brown Field."

"When?" Shiffon hadn't seen Maverick since they went their separate ways. At least once a day she replayed their last conversation, when she divulged Genesis had rehired her to kill him.

"Tomorrow. I don't know the exact time but I believe late afternoon. But of course get there early, so you have enough time to catch that nigga and blow his fuckin' brains out before he boards that flight."

"I thought I was off that job?"

"Consider yo'self back on. It's a good thing you went home to Atlanta or we woulda missed his ass. It worked out," Caleb said, itching for Maverick to die. "Now all you have to do is show up and make the kill."

"Consider myself on it," Shiffon said, trying to convince herself she could deliver.

"Good. Call me when it's done. I gotta go, someone's at the door." Caleb hung up wondering who the fuck it could be. "Mia, what are you doing here?"

"I'm sorry for just popping up over here but your number was disconnected and I really needed to get in touch with you. Have you spoken to Prevan or your mother?"

"No...why?" Caleb answered letting Mia in.

"Then I guess that means you haven' heard."

"Heard what?"

"Celinda, she's dead." Mia waited for Caleb's

reaction but he stood there and said nothing. "Did you hear what I said?"

"Yeah, I heard you. How is Amelia?"

"She's taking it hard but she's been staying with your Mother, so she'll be okay."

"And Prevan?"

"Of course he's hurt."

"And you…are you okay?"

"I'm better now."

"Better now." Caleb raised an eyebrow, thinking that was an odd choice of words. "So what happened…how to Mia die?" he couldn't stand her but Caleb was curious to know.

Instead of answering his question. Mia decided to pronounce her undying love for Caleb. "I love you, Caleb. I always have. I truly believe in my heart, I'm the woman you need."

"Mia, let's not do this right now." Caleb sat down on the couch, trying to wrap his mind around the fact Celinda was dead.

"But we have to. You're the reason my sister is dead."

"I didn't fuckin' kill her. Yeah, I wanted her dead but…"

"But you couldn't do it," Mia said interrupting Caleb. "That's why I did it for you…for us."

"Yo, what tha fuck are you talkin' about!"

Caleb was leaned forward with his elbows pressed on his lower thighs and his hands against the side of his temple. He felt a slight throbbing in his head.

Mia walked over to Caleb and kneeled down staring him in the eyes. "My sister was poison to all of us, especially you. Celinda had to be dealt with and now we can be together."

"Mia, what did you do?"

"The same way I described my sister as being poison, it seemed only right she died from what she was."

Mia could see Caleb staring at her with confusion in his eyes. He wasn't digesting what she was telling him, or maybe he didn't want to believe that sweet, innocent Mia was capable of murdering her own sister.

"Are you telling me you killed Celinda?"

"That's exactly what I'm telling you. I put what I learned from majoring in chemistry and interning at a lab, to murder my sister by poison," she explained very nonchalantly as if giving the recipe to her favorite dessert. "I did it for you Caleb." Mia placed her hand under Caleb's chin and kissed him, then whispered in his ear. "I would do anything for you."

"Mia, this is..."

She put her finger over his lips. "Don't speak. Just give me this moment. I deserve it, after what I did for you. I gave you what you wanted without leaving blood on your hands. Freeing you of any guilt."

Caleb couldn't decide if Mia was crazy or just crazy in love. His gut told him to tell her to get out but then he found himself drawn to the fact that she was willing to kill for him and he didn't even have to ask her to do so. But then Mia stood up and started undressing. Drawn turned into arousal when she slipped out her lace bra and panties. She crawled towards him naked, tugged at the drawstring on his joggers, pulling them down, so she could wrap her lips around Caleb's hardened dick.

Mia was a virgin and had never sucked a dick in her life. But she read and studied like she did for every chemistry test. Mia took it one step further and watched countless hours of porno videos, determined to get her skills just right. She knew she would only have one opportunity to make Caleb hers and Mia was determined not to fuck it up. Based on the grip he had on her hair and the deep moans Caleb was making, Mia felt she aced the test.

Chapter Twenty

Letting Go

One of the most difficult lessons in life is learning how to let go. Whether it's guilt, anger, love, loss or betrayal. Change is never easy. We fight to hold on and we fight to let go. For the last hour Shiffon had been at war with herself, trying to figure out if she had the courage to let Maverick go, while waiting for him to arrive. She knew once she pulled the trigger, he would be gone forever. She wasn't sure if she could live with that or even wanted to. Shiffon turned up the radio, so she could hear the lyrics to the song playing.

Un-thinkable (I'm Ready)

You give me a feeling that I never felt before
And I deserve it, I think I deserve it
It's becoming something that's impossible to
ignore
And I can't take it

I wondering, maybe
Could I make you my baby?
If we do the un-thinkable
Would it make us look crazy?
(Make us look crazy)

If you ask me, I'm ready...

Shiffon turned the volume down and closed her eyes. "You have a job to do," she said out loud, trying to pump herself up. "Stop living in a fantasy world and do what the fuck you were hired to do." She took a deep breath and opened her eyes. "And that time might be now," she sighed pulling out her binoculars.

Shiffon was parked at a somewhat far distance, to guarantee not being seen. She could see two SUV's pulling up, and assumed one of those SUV's had her target as a passenger. The Cessna Citation X aircraft was already on the tarmac.

She quickly grabbed her guns and descended towards her mark.

"Sir, would you like me to put your luggage on the aircraft?" the driver asked Maverick as he was wrapping up his phone call.

"Give me one sec," Maverick said to his caller. "Yeah, load the luggage," he told the driver. "But let the pilot know I'll be ready to leave shortly."

"Will do, sir," the driver said opening the trunk.

Maverick got back to his call but again had to press pause when he was interrupted by Cam knocking on the glass. "What's up?" he asked rolling down the window.

"You ready to roll? We already late," Cam told him.

"That's one of the reasons I chartered a plane, so I would be on my own fuckin' time!" Maverick exclaimed. "You and Micah go ahead and board the jet. Get comfortable. There's plenty of liquor and food. Let me finish this call and then we can go."

"Cool," Cam nodded.

Shiffon lurked in the background watching everyone board the flight. All seemed to be accounted for besides Maverick, which meant he was still in the SUV. When she knew he was alone, she came out the darkness and made her move. Shiffon's heart was racing. She always got an adrenaline rush when she was about to kill someone but this felt different. She was about to put a bullet in the man she loved. When the door opened and Maverick stepped out, she immediately aimed her gun at the back of his head.

"If you gonna shoot, then do it." Maverick stated without turning around. "But I prefer you lookin' me in the eye before I die," he said now facing Shiffon.

"If you knew I waiting for you, why did you get out?" Shiffon asked

"Because I wanted to see if you would actually go through with it and kill me. When I gave you the chance before, you couldn't do it. Are you ready to do it now?" Maverick took a few steps closer, as if daring Shiffon to kill him.

Shiffon tightened the grip on her gun, not letting go. "Don't come any closer, Maverick. "I will pull the trigger," she warned.

"Then do it. But make sure you ready to watch me die. You'll never see me again. Is that what you want because it's not what I want."

"It was you...it was you who was watching me. I felt it," Shiffon swallowed, thinking back to when her and Essence were coming out of Lennox Mall.

"Of course it was me. I didn't have to charter a private plane from Atlanta. I wanted to see you again before I left," Maverick admitted.

"You also wanted to see if I would track you down and kill you."

"That too," he acknowledged.

"You're playing a dangerous game," Shiffon said, thinking to herself, this wasn't a game she was prepared to play.

"I know. Is there any other sort of game to play? So which will it be. Are you gonna kill me or board that flight and leave with me? The ball is in your court."

Maverick's options seemed like a lose-lose to Shiffon. Her heart was no longer racing it was her mind going crazy. Did she kill the man she loved or disappear with him. The choice was hers and Shiffon needed to make her decision now.

"I don't think I can do this," Aaliyah said to Angel as they stood outside Nico's hospital room.

"I know. I was tempted to fight it. Get the best lawyer in New York City and drag it out but then I thought about our father. He would never want to live, if it required a machine to make it possible. Once I accepted that, I knew we had to let him go," Angel said sadly.

"You're right. I'm really sorry, Angel." Aaliyah placed her hands on top of Angel's.

"Why are you apologizing to me?"

"Because I had our father in my life since I was a little girl but you...you only had him for such a short period of time. You didn't get to see just how amazing he is," Aaliyah cried.

"You're wrong, I did get to see just how amazing he is. From the moment he found out I was his daughter, he embraced me and loved me, like I had been in his life forever. Amazing doesn't do him justice. He changed my life for the better and he also gave me the best big sister," Angel smiled, hugging Aaliyah.

"Ditto. Are you ready?" Aaliyah asked Angel, wiping the tears and pulling herself together.

"Yes. I'm ready." Angel did her best to appear resolute. They held hands and walked into their Father's hospital room together.

Precious, Supreme, Lorenzo, T-Roc and Genesis were all there. They stood around Nico's bed in a deep gaze. He appeared to be resting peacefully. They all wanted to remember him that way; not in pain but at peace. In their minds each replaying the best and worst moments they shared with the great Nico Carter.

"It's time." The doctor walked in and announced.

Precious leaned down and whispered in Nico's ear. "You were my first love and I will forever hold you in my heart." Precious gave Nico a goodbye kiss before the doctor pulled the plug.

Coming Soon!!

Bad Bitches Only

ASSASSINS...

EPISODE 1
(Be Careful With Me)

JOY DEJA KING

A KING PRODUCTION

Chapter One

HE LOVES ME

Bailey strutted out the Hartsfield-Jackson Atlanta International Airport, in her strappy, four inch snakeskin shoes, wearing matte black wire frame square sunglas ses and a designer suit tailored to fit her size six frame perfectly. The brown beauty looked like she was a partner at a powerful law firm, when actually she was barely a second year law student. But school was the least of her worries. Bailey had other things on her mind, like the promise ring she was wearing. It cost more than some people's home. Don't get it confused, this wasn't a promise of sexual abstinence. This was a promise of marriage, from her boyfriend of five years, Dino Jacobs.

"Keera," I was just about to call you girl," Bailey said, getting in her car.

"I was shocked as shit when you answered. I was expecting to leave a voicemail. You said you was gonna be in some conferences all day," Keera replied.

"Girl, I was but I checked out early. I'm back in the A."

"You back in Atlanta?!" Keera questioned, sounding surprised.

"Yep. That's why I was calling you. So we could do drinks later on tonight at that spot we like." Baily was getting hyped, as she was dropping the top on her Lunar Blue Metallic E 400 Benz.

"Most definitely...so where you headed now."

"Where you think...home to my man! Stop playin'," Bailey laughed, getting on interstate 75.

"I know yo' boo, will be happy to see you."

"Yep and his ass gon' be surprised too. He thinks I'm coming back tomorrow night. But I missed my baby. Plus that conference was boring as hell. All them snobby ass lawyers was workin' my nerves."

"Get used to it, cause you about to be one," Keera reminded her.

"Yeah but only cause Dino insisted. You know

I wanted to attend beauty school. I love all things hair and makeup. I have zero interest in law. But that nigga the one paying for it, so it's whatever," Bailey smacked.

"Girl, don't be wasting that man money. You better get yo' law degree and handle them cases!" Keera giggled.

"Okaaaay!! I believe Dino just want me to be able to represent his ass, in case anything go down," Bailey snickered.

"Well, let me get off the phone so you can get home."

"Keera, I know how to talk and drive at the same damn time," she popped.

"I didn't say you didn't but umm I have a nail appointment. You know they be swamped on a Friday," Keera explained.

"True. Okay, go get yo' raggedy nails done," Bailey joked. "Call me later, so we can decide what time we meeting for drinks."

"Will do! Talk to you later on."

When Bailey got off the phone with Keera, she immediately started blasting some Cardi B. The music, mixed with the nice summer breeze blowing through her hair, had her feeling sexy. She began imagining the dick down she'd get from Dino, soon as she got home.

"Here I come baby," Bailey smiled, pulling in the driveway. She was practically skipping inside the house and up the stairs, giddy like a silly schoolgirl. You'd think hearing Silk's old school Freak Me, echoing down the hallway, in the middle of the afternoon, would've sent the alarm ringing in Bailey's head. Instead, it made her try to reach her man faster.

It wasn't until she got a few steps from the slightly ajar bedroom door, did her heart start racing. Next came the rapid breathing and finally came dread. You know the type of dread, that seems like it's worse than death but you don't know for sure because you've never actually died. It was all too much for Bailey. Her eyes were bleeding blood. She wanted to erase everything she just witnessed and rewind time.

I shoulda kept my ass in DC, she screamed to herself, heading back downstairs and leaving the house. Once outside, Bailey started to vomit in the bushes, until there was nothing left in her stomach.

A KING PRODUCTION

Bad Bitches Only

ASSASSINS...

EPISODE 2
(Clout Chasers)

JOY DEJA KING

A KING PRODUCTION

Bad Bitches Only

ASSASSINS...

EPISODE 3
(Killing The King)

JOY DEJA KING

Read The Entire Bitch Series in This Order

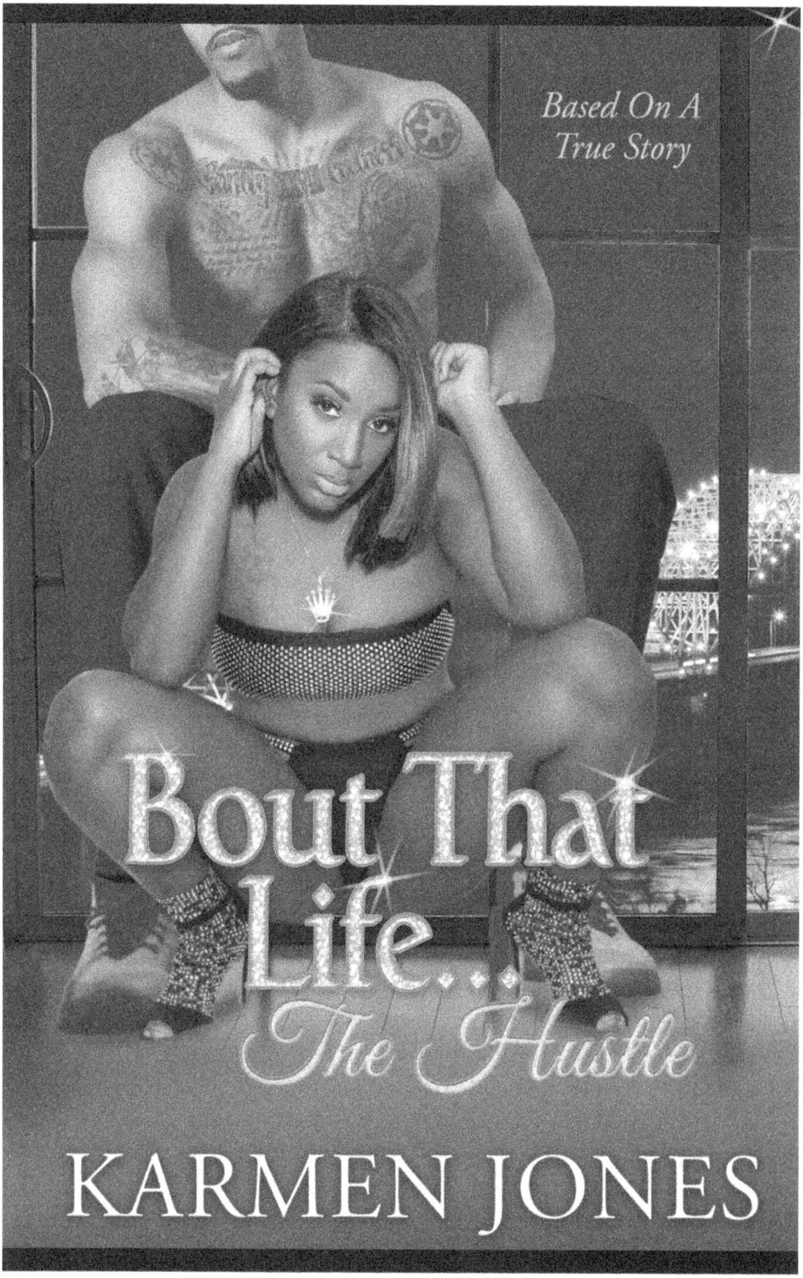
Based On A
True Story
Bout That
Life...
The Hustle
KARMEN JONES

ORDER FORM

Name:

Address:

City/State:

Zip:

QUANTITY	TITLES	PRICE	TOTAL
	Bitch	$15.00	
	Bitch Reloaded	$15.00	
	The Bitch Is Back	$15.00	
	Queen Bitch	$15.00	
	Last Bitch Standing	$15.00	
	Superstar	$15.00	
	Ride Wit' Me	$12.00	
	Ride Wit' Me Part 2	$15.00	
	Stackin' Paper	$15.00	
	Trife Life To Lavish	$15.00	
	Trife Life To Lavish II	$15.00	
	Stackin' Paper II	$15.00	
	Rich or Famous	$15.00	
	Rich or Famous Part 2	$15.00	
	Rich or Famous Part 3	$15.00	
	Bitch A New Beginning	$15.00	
	Mafia Princess Part 1	$15.00	
	Mafia Princess Part 2	$15.00	
	Mafia Princess Part 3	$15.00	
	Mafia Princess Part 4	$15.00	
	Mafia Princess Part 5	$15.00	
	Boss Bitch	$15.00	
	Baller Bitches Vol. 1	$15.00	
	Baller Bitches Vol. 2	$15.00	
	Baller Bitches Vol. 3	$15.00	
	Bad Bitch	$15.00	
	Still The Baddest Bitch	$15.00	
	Power	$15.00	
	Power Part 2	$15.00	
	Drake	$15.00	
	Drake Part 2	$15.00	
	Female Hustler	$15.00	
	Female Hustler Part 2	$15.00	
	Female Hustler Part 3	$15.00	
	Female Hustler Part 4	$15.00	
	Female Hustler Part 5	$15.00	
	Female Hustler Part 6	$15.00	
	Princess Fever "Birthday Bash"	$6.00	
	Nico Carter The Men Of The Bitch Series	$15.00	
	Bitch The Beginning Of The End	$15.00	
	Supreme...Men Of The Bitch Series	$15.00	
	Bitch The Final Chapter	$15.00	
	Stackin' Paper III	$15.00	
	Men Of The Bitch Series And The Women Who Love Them	$15.00	
	Coke Like The 80s	$15.00	
	Baller Bitches The Reunion Vol. 4	$15.00	
	Stackin' Paper IV	$15.00	
	The Legacy	$15.00	
	Lovin' Thy Enemy	$15.00	
	Stackin' Paper V	$15.00	
	The Legacy Part 2	$15.00	
	Assassins - Episode 1	$11.00	
	Assassins - Episode 2	$11.00	
	Assassins - Episode 2	$11.00	
	Bitch Chronicles	$40.00	
	So Hood So Rich	$15.00	
	Stackin' Paper VI	$17.99	

Shipping/Handling (Via Priority Mail) $7.50 1-2 Books, $15.00 3-4 Books add $1.95 for ea. Additional book.

Total: $_____ FORMS OF ACCEPTED PAYMENTS: Certified or government issued checks and money Orders, all mail in orders take 5-7 Business days to be delivered

CPSIA information can be obtained
at www.ICGtesting.com
Printed in the USA
LVHW051658300120
645335LV00003B/389